"Otsuka beautifully renders the particularities of a life fully using every word, including the pronouns. She has a way of presenting seemingly objective details, but the emotions seep through the minutiae so that we know and feel much about Alice and those who care for her.... *The Swimmers* is [an] artfully refined story, even when it delves into the most painful parts of life."

—*Minneapolis Star Tribune*

"[*The Swimmers*] offers satirical comment on contemporary life with nimble precision. . . . Julie Otsuka finds a deft humor in each observation."

—*Los Angeles Review of Books*

"There are books that seem as if they were written just for me, and Julie Otsuka's *The Swimmers* is one of them.... Otsuka [is] taking the gloves off in a way she hasn't since the ending of *When the Emperor Was Divine*."

—Alice Stephens,
Washington Independent Review of Books

"A quick and tender story of a group of swimmers who cope with the disruption of their routines in various ways. . . . It's a brilliant and disarming dive into the characters' inner worlds."

—*Publishers Weekly* (starred review)

"Julie Otsuka's first novel in ten years is a quiet and startling masterpiece about memory, aging and the indelible experiences that define a life. . . . Funny, moving and composed of sentences that read like small poems, *The Swimmers* is a remarkable novel from a writer with an unparalleled talent for capturing the stuff of the world, whether mundane, harrowing or bizarre."

—*BookPage* (starred review)

"Award-winning, bestselling Otsuka is averaging one book per decade, making each exquisite title exponentially more precious. Here she creates a stupendous collage of small moments that results in an extraordinary examination of the fragility of quotidian human relationships. . . . Once more, Otsuka creates an elegiac, devastating masterpiece."

—*Booklist* (starred review)

JULIE OTSUKA

The Swimmers

Julie Otsuka was born and raised in California. She is the recipient of a Guggenheim Fellowship, and her first novel, *When the Emperor Was Divine*, published in 2002, won the Asian American Literary Award and the American Library Association Alex Award. Her second novel, *The Buddha in the Attic*, published in 2011, was a finalist for the National Book Award and won the PEN/Faulkner Award for Fiction. *The Buddha in the Attic* was an international bestseller and the winner of the Prix Femina étranger and the Albatros Literaturpreis. She lives in New York City.

julieotsuka.com

ALSO BY JULIE OTSUKA

The Buddha in the Attic

When the Emperor Was Divine

The Swimmers

The Swimmers

JULIE OTSUKA

ANCHOR BOOKS
A DIVISION OF PENGUIN RANDOM HOUSE LLC
NEW YORK

FIRST ANCHOR BOOKS EDITION 2023

"Diem Perdidi" was originally published in slightly different form in *Granta* (granta.com) on October 27, 2011.

The Library of Congress has cataloged the Knopf edition as follows:
Names: Otsuka, Julie, [date] author.
Title: The swimmers / Julie Otsuka.
Description: First edition. | New York : Alfred A. Knopf, 2022.
Identifiers: LCCN 2021035576 (print) | LCCN 2021035577 (ebook)
Subjects: LCGFT: Novels.
Classification: LCC PS3615.T88 S95 2022 (print) | LCC PS3615.T88 (ebook) | DDC 813/.6—dc23
LC record available at https://lccn.loc.gov/2021035576
LC ebook record available at https://lccn.loc.gov/2021035577

Anchor Books Trade Paperback ISBN: 978-0-593-46662-9
eBook ISBN: 978-0-593-32134-8

Title page image: based on an image by Cozine/stock.adobe.com
Book design by Pei Loi Koay

anchorbooks.com

Printed in the United States of America
2nd Printing

For Andy

The Swimmers

THE UNDERGROUND POOL

The pool is located deep underground, in a large cavernous chamber many feet beneath the streets of our town. Some of us come here because we are injured, and need to heal. We suffer from bad backs, fallen arches, shattered dreams, broken hearts, anxiety, melancholia, anhedonia, the usual above-ground afflictions. Others of us are employed at the college nearby and prefer to take our lunch breaks down below, in the waters, far away from the harsh glares of our colleagues and screens. Some of us come here to escape, if only for an hour, our disappointing marriages on land. Many of us live in the neighborhood and simply love to swim. One of us—Alice, a retired lab technician now in the early stages of dementia—comes here because she always has. And even though she may not remember the combination to her locker or where she put her towel, the moment she slips into the water she knows what to do. Her stroke is long and fluid, her kick is strong, her mind clear. "Up there," she says, "I'm just another little old lady. But down here, at the pool, I'm myself."

MOST DAYS, AT THE POOL, we are able to leave our troubles on land behind. Failed painters become elegant breaststrokers. Untenured professors slice, sharklike, through the water, with breathtaking speed. The newly divorced HR Manager grabs a faded red Styrofoam board and kicks with impunity. The downsized adman floats, otter-like, on his back, as he stares up at the clouds on the painted pale blue ceiling, thinking, for the first time all day long, of nothing. *Let it go.* Worriers stop worrying. Bereaved widows cease to grieve. Out-of-work actors unable to get traction above ground glide effortlessly down the fast lane, in their element, at last. *I've arrived!* And for a brief interlude we are at home in the world. Bad moods lift, tics disappear, memories reawaken, migraines dissolve, and slowly, slowly, the chatter in our minds begins to subside as stroke after stroke, length after length, we swim. And when we are finished with our laps we hoist ourselves up out of the pool, dripping and refreshed, our equilibrium restored, ready to face another day on land.

UP ABOVE THERE ARE wildfires, smog alerts, epic droughts, paper jams, teachers' strikes, insurrections, revolutions, blisteringly hot days that never seem to let up (*Massive "Heat Dome" Permanently Stalled over Entire West Coast*), but down below, at the pool, it is always a comfortable eighty-one degrees. The humidity is sixty-five percent. The visibility is clear. The lanes are orderly and calm. The hours, though limited, are adequate for our needs. Some of us arrive shortly upon waking, fresh towels draped over our shoulders and rubber goggles in hand, ready for our eight a.m. swim. Others of us come down in the late afternoon, after work, when it is still sunny and bright, and when we reemerge it is night. The traffic has thinned. The backhoes have quieted. The birds have all gone away. And we are grateful to have avoided, once more, the falling of dusk. *It's the one time I can't bear being alone.* Some of us come to the pool religiously, five times a week, and begin to feel guilty if we miss even a day. Some of us come every Monday, Wednesday and Friday at noon. One of us comes a half hour before closing and by the time she changes into her suit and gets into the water it's time to get out. Another of us is dying of Parkinson's disease and just comes when he can. *If I'm here then you know I'm having a good day.*

THE RULES AT THE POOL, though unspoken, are adhered to by all (we are our own best enforcers): no running, no shouting, no children allowed. Circle swimming only (direction counterclockwise, always keeping to the right of the painted black line). All Band-Aids must be removed. No one who has not taken the compulsory two-minute shower (hot water, soap) in the locker room may enter the pool. No one who has an unexplained rash or open wound may enter the pool (the menstruating among us, however, are excepted). No one who is not a member of the pool may enter the pool. Guests are permitted (no more than one per member at a time), but for a nominal daily fee. Bikinis are permitted but not encouraged. Bathing caps are required. Cell phones are forbidden. Proper pool etiquette must be observed at all times. If you cannot keep up the pace you must stop at the end of your lane to let the swimmer behind you pass. If you want to pass someone from behind you must tap them once on the foot to warn them. If you accidentally bump into another swimmer you must check to make sure that they are all right. Be nice to Alice. Obey the lifeguard at all times. Turn your head at regular intervals and remember, of course, to breathe.

IN OUR "REAL LIVES," up above, we are overeaters, underachievers, dog walkers, cross-dressers, compulsive knitters (*Just one more row*), secret hoarders, minor poets, trailing spouses, twins, vegans, "Mom," a second-rate fashion designer, an undocumented immigrant, a nun, a Dane, a cop, an actor who just plays a cop on TV ("Officer Mahoney"), a winner of the green card lottery, a two-time nominee for Outstanding Professor of the Year, a nationally ranked go player, three guys named George (George the podiatrist, George the nephew of the disgraced financier, George the former welterweight Golden Gloves boxer), two Roses (Rose, and the Other Rose), one Ida, one Alice, one self-described nobody (*Don't mind me*), one former member of the SDS, two convicted felons, addicted, enabled, embattled, embittered, out of print, out of luck (*I think I just seroconverted*), in the twilight of lackluster real estate careers, in the middle of long and protracted divorces (*It's year seven*), infertile, in our prime, in a rut, in a rush, in remission, in the third week of chemo, in deep and unrelenting emotional despair (*You never get used to it*), but down below, at the pool, we are only one of three things: fast-lane people, medium-lane people or the slow.

THE FAST-LANE PEOPLE are the alpha people of the pool. They are high-strung and aggressive and supremely confident in their stroke. They look excellent in their swimsuits. Anatomically, they tend to be mesomorphs who carry an extra pound or two of fat for enhanced flotation. They have broad shoulders and long torsos and are equally divided between women and men. Whenever they kick, the water churns and boils. It is best to stay out of their way. They are natural-born athletes blessed with both rhythm and speed and have an uncanny feel for the water that the rest of us lack.

THE MEDIUM-LANE PEOPLE are visibly more relaxed than their fast-lane brethren. They come in all sizes and shapes and have long ago given up any dreams they may have once harbored of swimming in a faster and better lane. No matter how hard they try, it's not going to happen, and they know it. Every once in a while, however, one of them will succumb to a bout of furious kicking, a sudden and involuntary windmilling of the arms and legs as though they thought, for a moment, that they could somehow defy their fate. But the moment never lasts for long. Legs soon tire out, strokes shorten, elbows droop, lungs begin to ache, and after a length or two they return to their normal everyday pace. *That's just the way it is,* they say to themselves. And then amiably, affably—*Just pulling your leg, guys!*—they swim on.

THE SLOW-LANE PEOPLE tend to be older men who have recently retired, women over the age of forty-nine, water walkers, aqua joggers, visiting economists from landlocked emerging third-world countries where, we have heard, they are only just now learning how to swim (*It's the same with their driving*), and the occasional patient in rehab. Be kind to them. Make no assumptions. There are many reasons they might be here: arthritis, sciatica, insomnia, a brand-new titanium hip, aching feet worn out from a lifetime of pounding on dry land. "My mother *told* me never to wear high heels!" The pool is their sanctuary, their refuge, the one place on earth they can go to escape from their pain, for it is only down below, in the waters, that their symptoms begin to abate. *The moment I see that painted black line I feel fine.*

ABOVE GROUND MANY of us are ungainly and awkward, slowing down with the years. The extra poundage has arrived, the letting go has begun, the crow's-feet are fanning out silently, but inexorably, like cracks on a windshield, from the corners of our eyes. But down below, at the pool, we are restored to our old youthful selves. Gray hairs vanish beneath dark blue swim caps. Brows unfurrow. Limps disappear. Kettle-bellied men with knee woes on land bob daintily up and down in their bright orange flotation belts as they aqua-jog in place. Plus-sized women well past their prime grow supple and agile in the water, dolphin-sleek in their figure-slimming Spandex suits. Stomachs are flattened. Bosoms lifted. Long-lost waistlines reemerge. *There it is!* Even the most rotund of us steers her majestic bulk down her lane with ease and aplomb, as though she were the stately *Queen Mary*. *This body of mine was built to float!* And those of us who would normally bemoan our sagging visages on land—*Every year it gets harder and harder to keep up the face*—glide serenely through the water, safe in our knowledge that we are nothing more than a blurry peripheral shape glimpsed in passing through the foggy tinted goggles of the swimmer in the next lane.

PEOPLE TO WATCH out for: aggressive lappers, determined thrashers, oblivious backstrokers, stealthy submariners, middle-aged men who insist upon speeding up the moment they sense they are about to be overtaken by a woman, tailgaters, lane Nazis, arm flailers, ankle yankers, the pickup artist (we are not that kind of a pool), the peeper (a highly regarded children's TV host in his life above ground who is best known belowground for his swift lane change—*Nubile new female swimmer in lane four!*—and his "accidental" underwater bump: *So sorry*), the woman in lane four with the wide, overextended stroke (too much yoga), the former three-time Olympian (two silver medals, hundred-meter medley relay; one bronze, hundred-meter backstroke) who is now in her second year at the medical school and appears so much different in real life than she did on the TV. "I thought she'd be bigger" is the disappointed refrain that can often be heard following one of her unannounced visits. Sightings of the Olympian are rare. She comes down, she dives in, she swims—leisurely, languidly, with no apparent effort at all, although every one of her strokes carries her three times as far as one of ours—and then she returns to her life above. Do not disturb her. Do not ask for her autograph. She is our Garbo, and prefers to be left alone.

THERE ARE CERTAIN members of our community you will encounter only in the locker room, but never in the pool itself: the frequent flosser (women's locker room, middle sink, appears like clockwork three times a day), the toilet paper thief (men's locker room, once a week, never takes more than he needs), the mirror checker ("Do I look okay?" this person will ask you, to which you must reply, enthusiastically, "Yes, you look great!"), the meticulous shaver (sometimes takes an entire morning to remove every last whisker from his face), the heavyset woman in mismatched flip-flops who stands beneath the shower for hours with her eyes closed, head flung back, legs spread wide apart, soaping herself furiously, frantically, as though it were her one and only chance to get clean. These people are harmless. They have their reasons for being here, as do we. Do not be alarmed by their presence. Do not make fun of them. Work around them, if you can. For they have been coming here for years without causing us any trouble and to interfere with them now would surely bring us bad luck in the lanes.

THE LIFEGUARD ENTERS the pool through a separate entrance marked STAFF ONLY and sits atop a high metal stool in front of the wooden bleachers, gazing out across the water for hours. The lifeguard wears white shorts and a light blue shirt and reports directly to the Aquatics Director, a small, bespectacled man in a battered windbreaker whose windowless office sits opposite the vending machines on the lower-mezzanine landing. The lifeguard is sometimes a skinny teenage boy and sometimes a grown man. Occasionally, the lifeguard is a young woman. Often, the lifeguard is late. Timely or tardy, young or old, male or female, the lifeguard never lasts for long. Last month, the lifeguard was an out-of-work IT guy from the next town over. The month before that, the local football coach's son. *Land people,* we say. This month, the lifeguard is a dark-haired man of indeterminate age who always has a radio pressed close to his ear. It is impossible to know what, if anything, he is thinking. To our friendly hellos, he responds with a barely perceptible nod. Rumors about the new lifeguard are rife. He is twenty-seven. He is fifty-eight. He is weeping. He is sleeping. He doesn't really *care.* He would always, we suspect, rather be elsewhere. For it is with visible relief—and, some would say, barely suppressed glee—that he blows his whistle at the end of every session and shouts out, in a faint yet audible accent of vaguely eastern European origin, our two least favorite words: "Everybody out!"

OUR FIRST FEW moments back on land are always the hardest. The too-bright sun beating down through the tattered canopy of the trees. The insufferably blue skies. The worried-looking men in dark suits hurriedly getting in and out of their cars. The thin, exhausted mothers. The little white dogs viciously lunging and snapping at the ends of their long retractable leashes. *Freddie, no!* The sirens. The jackhammers. The unnaturally green lawns. We take a deep breath as we toss our damp towels cavalierly over our shoulders and put down one heavy foot after the other and plod, wet-haired and wobbly-kneed, deep grooves from our goggles still circling our eyes, from Point A to Point B. *I'm back!* And even though it is with reluctance that we return to our lives above, we take it all in stride, for we are mere day-trippers here, in the realm of the upper air.

LATE AT NIGHT, as we are falling asleep, we begin to go over our form in our heads. Our elbows could be higher, our legs straighter (*Kick from the hip, not the knee!*), our shoulders more relaxed. We picture ourselves pushing hard off the wall with our toes pointed and our bodies fully extended and then rolling to one side as we move into the stroke. *Imagine you are reaching over a barrel.* Our torsos are streamlined. Our ankles are loose. Our attitude, upbeat yet serene. *It's just water.* We practice our breathing, inhaling great lungfuls of air through our noses and mouths and then pursing our lips and slowly blowing it all out. We pull our blankets up over our heads and whisper our words silently into our pillows: *Align the head and spine, align the head and spine.* Dutifully, but reluctantly, we revisit our past mistakes. *I was holding my breath for years.* When our partners—those of us who have them—reach over sleepily and ask us what it is that's on our minds, we tell them "Nothing" or "Is tomorrow recycling?" or "Why do you think those dinosaurs *really* disappeared?" But we never say, "The pool." Because the pool is ours and ours alone. *It's my own secret Valhalla.*

IF TOO MUCH TIME is spent up above we become uncharacteristically curt with our colleagues, we slip up on our programs, we are rude to waiters even though one of us—lane seven, little black Speedo, enormous, flipper-like feet—is a waiter himself, we cease to delight our mates. *Not now.* And even though we do our best to resist the urge to descend—*It'll pass,* we tell ourselves—we can feel our panic beginning to rise, as though we were somehow missing out on our own lives. *Just a quick dip and everything will be all right.* And when we can stand it no longer we politely excuse ourselves from whatever it is we're doing—discussing this month's book with our book club, celebrating an office birthday, ending an affair, wandering aimlessly up and down the fluorescent-lit aisles of the local Safeway trying to remember what it was we came in to buy (*Mallomars? Lorna Doones?*)—and go down for a swim. Because there's no place on earth we'd rather be than the pool: its wide roped-off lanes, clearly numbered one through eight, its deep, well-designed gutters, its cheerful yellow buoys spaced at pleasingly predictable intervals, its separate but equal entrances for women and men, the warm ambient glow of its recessed overhead lights, all provide us with a sense of comfort and order that is missing from our aboveground lives.

THE SHOCK OF the water—there is nothing like it on land. The cool clear liquid flowing over every inch of your skin. The temporary reprieve from gravity. The miracle of your own buoyancy as you glide, unhindered, across the glossy blue surface of the pool. *It's just like flying.* The pure pleasure of being in motion. The dissipation of all want. *I'm free.* You are suddenly aloft. Adrift. Ecstatic. Euphoric. In a rapturous and trancelike state of bliss. And if you swim for long enough you no longer know where your own body ends and the water begins and there is no boundary between you and the world. *It's nirvana.*

SOME OF US have to swim one hundred laps every day, others, sixty-eight (one mile) or one hundred and two (a mile and a half), or for exactly forty-five minutes (Eduardo, lane six), or until the bad thoughts go away (Sister Catherine, lane two). One of us does not trust his own counting and always swims an extra lap or two every time "just to make sure." One of us always loses count after five. One of us (Professor Weng Wei Li, author of *The Solace of Primes*) prefers to swim exactly eighty-nine. One of us swears she hits her bliss point the moment she glides into lap fifty-three. "Happens every time." All of us have our rituals. One of us has to glance—casually—at the red hand on the laminated Larceny Alert poster in the stairwell before jumping into the pool. One of us has to take three sips from the rusty water fountain before jumping into the pool, despite—or, some would say, because of ("I'm a risk taker!")—his fear of lead in the pipes. One of us refuses to swim in her usual lane (lane seven) if her ex-husband is swimming in lane eight. One of us is her "new" husband of five and a half years and for the past five and a half years he has been swimming contentedly in lane six ("I know my place"), pretending not to notice a thing. "Let them work it out." There are adamant preswim stretchers among us, and others—equally adamant—who insist that postswim is best. There is a backstroker in lane four who cannot get out of the pool until he has touched his cap twice and then counted to five. "I don't know why." There is Alice, who cannot be bothered with counting and just swims till she's done.

IF YOU HAVE a complaint—someone is talking animatedly in a too-loud tone of voice, the clock has stopped, there is a slow swimmer in the fast lane, a fast swimmer in the slow lane, your favorite Monopoly-board-patterned towel has disappeared from the locker room, your shoulder hurts, your goggles are leaking, your hairstylist has gone *insane*—do not bring it to the attention of the lifeguard. Because nine times out of ten, the lifeguard will do nothing. Feel free, however, to take matters into your own hands. Do a few shoulder stretches. Find a new salon. At the risk of sounding petty, put up a sign: *Who stole my towel?* Confront the loud talker politely but firmly and ask that person to please tone it down. Or, if you wish, you may report the rule breaker directly to management by writing down the offender's name on a piece of paper and dropping it into the metal suggestion box (a.k.a. the "mailbox for denunciations") on the Aquatics Director's door. Be aware, however, that from that moment on you will risk being known as a turncoat and the object of our silent scorn. Conversations will stop in your presence. "That's *her*." Locker room buddies will cease saying hello. Naked and less-than-pretty backsides will forever be turned your way. And one day, when you step out of the shower, you may discover that your swimsuit, too, has mysteriously disappeared. So think twice before pointing the finger at a fellow swimmer and bringing upon them the worst fate of all: permanent and irrevocable expulsion from the underground pool.

FLIP TURNS. Some of us can do them, but many of us cannot. "Too scary," says one of us. Another says they aggravate his lower back. A number of us aspire to them—"It's on my to-do list"—while others shun the very thought. "I tried one once and thought I was going to drown." One of us always fears she'll start her turn too late and smash her head into the wall. "And yet I never have." One of us is a former All-American whose stylishly savage turns are the envy of us all. *He's got just the right amount of splash.* One of us recently mastered her flip turn at the age of sixty-three. "It's never too late!" One of us learned how to turn several decades ago and even though she has slowed down considerably on her approach to the wall the muscle memory is still encoded deep in the synapses of her brain. "It's just a somersault with a twist." One of us is overly prideful of his "fast, killer" turn—"It's the thing about myself I like best"—while others feign nonchalance. "What's the big deal?" we say, and "Really, who *cares?*" for we are here at the pool, after all, not to turn but to swim.

WE ARE THE first to admit that life down below has its drawbacks. There is no privacy down below, for example. And very little variety. *I've been swimming the backstroke in lane three every day for the past twenty-seven years.* And, with the exception of the spiral-bound membership manual tucked away beneath two half-eaten PowerBars on the bottom of a desk drawer in the Aquatics Commissioner's office, too few books.

Also, no esplanades, no horizons, no napping and, saddest of all, no sky. But, we are eager to point out, we also have no riptides, no jellyfish, no sunburns, no lightning, no internet, no nonsense, no riffraff and, best of all, no shoes. And what we lack in horizon and sky we make up for in tranquility, for one of the best things about the pool is the brief respite it offers us from the noisy world above: the hedge trimmers, the weed whackers, the horn honkers, the nose blowers, the throat clearers, the page rustlers, the incessant music that is playing wherever you go—at the dentist's office, at the drugstore, in the elevator taking you up to see the audiologist about that strange ringing in your ears. *Doc, please make it go away!* The minute you put your head down into the water, all that noise is gone. All you can hear is the soothing sound of your own breathing, the rhythmic rise and fall of your strokes, the muffled splash of your neighbor flutter-kicking away in the next lane and, every once in a while, an ethereal snatch of song drifting, dreamy and fog-like, through the thick chlorinated air: why it's Alice, singing "Dancing on the Ceiling," as she pulls on her white flowered cap. *The world is lyrical because a miracle . . .* But most of the time it's just you and your own thoughts as you glide through the cool, clear water.

ONE OF US, a health reporter at the *Daily Tribune* who is buoyantly pregnant with her fifth child at the age of forty-six, realized that her father had undiagnosed Huntington's disease while swimming her laps. *And all this time I thought he was crazy.* One of us composes his weekly astronomy lecture while swimming his laps, and when he is finished he climbs up out of the pool and into the bleachers and writes it all down on his dry yellow pad. *Greetings, earthlings,* he always begins. One of us has a photographic memory and solves the daily crossword puzzle every morning while swimming his laps. "If it takes me ten minutes I swim for ten minutes. If it takes me an hour I swim for an hour." One of us goes over her goals for the month while swimming her laps: *diversify portfolio, stop snacking, make ripples, leave Doug.* Alice stares down at the painted black line on the bottom of the pool while swimming her laps as scenes from her childhood flash one by one through her head. *I was jumping rope in the desert. I was looking for shells in the sand. I was checking under the raspberry bush to see if the chickens had laid any more eggs.* And even though she will not remember a thing once she returns to her life above, for the rest of the day she will feel enlivened and alert, as though she had been away on a long trip.

IF YOU RUN into a fellow member of the pool unexpectedly above ground you may find yourself blushing awkwardly, as though meeting for the first time, even though you may have seen this person every day, sopping wet, practically naked, for more than ten years. *I didn't recognize her in her clothes,* you may think to yourself. Or *His shirt is too tight.* Or *Age-inappropriate jeans!* And after that you'll never be able to look at this person in quite the same way again. Or maybe you'll find yourself staring at a stranger in the pharmacy with no idea why and then you'll suddenly realize, *It's the guy with the snorkel who always swims in lane three. He takes Lipitor too!* Or you'll be driving down to the mall and experience an intense moment of déjà vu as someone zips past you, cursing and shaking her head while she leans on her horn. Why, it's your lane mate, Suzette, in her fancy black BMW, passing you on land with the same courtesy as she does down below. "Yo, *Sue!*" you shout out as you step on the gas and give her a brief toot of your own. Or you'll catch a glimpse of Alice as she is coming out of Longs Drugs—*Her hair was disheveled and her pants were on inside out*—and you'll stop for a moment to ask if everything's all right. "Everything's great!" she'll say. "See you next time at the pool!" And the next time you see her she's back in top form, looking fabulous in her green-and-white smocked swimsuit as she extends one graceful arm after the other through the water and swims her tranquil liquid lengths.

AFTER NEW YEAR'S and other major holidays during which alarming quantities of food have been steadily ingested, you may notice a sudden influx of newcomers frantic to swim off the pounds. *Binge swimmers*, we call them. They dive in unshowered. They forget to wear their caps. They duck under the ropes and flit, insect-like, from one lane to the next. They are unkind to Alice. "Out of my way, lady." They pay no heed to our rules. If you tap them on the heel they are quick to turn around and take offense. "Hey, man, don't *touch*." More often than not, they are under the impression that they are fast. But after an initial display of swagger and speed they may suddenly come to a dead stop, midlength, and dangle from the ropes, panting and out of breath, bringing all traffic behind them to a halt. "Just taking a rest," they'll say. Try not to get angry with them. Defer judgment if you can. For they are temporary defilers of our waters, weak-willed interlopers who will not be with us for long. After a week or two they will lose all interest and the lanes will revert to their normal, less crowded state.

IT IS AN ILLUSION, of course, that the pool is ours and ours alone. We know that there are other users whose attachment to our waters is equally fierce. The triathlon swim trainers, for example, who practice every Sunday afternoon from four-thirty to six. Or the amateur divers club (Tuesdays and Thursdays from noon to one). Or the Tadpoles Swim Class for children under five (Saturdays from one to two). And if you forget about the time change and come down one day, say, at seven a.m. instead of eight, you will stumble upon the masters swim team doing their early-morning workout beneath the exacting eye of locally renowned Coach Vlad. *Pull! Pull! Pull!* And you may wonder, for a moment, as you stand there watching them streak torpedo-like up and down the lanes, their every stroke perfect, their timing exquisite, the slowest of their slow putting our fastest (former Olympian excepted) to shame, what you've been doing all these years. "I could have *sworn* I was swimming." Perhaps *they* are the real swimmers, and we are only pale facsimiles thereof. But quickly, quickly you put this thought out of your head as you close the heavy metal door behind you—*Mistake!*—and quietly walk away. And when you come back an hour later for your regular eight a.m. swim it's as if they were never there. The kickboards are neatly stacked by color in two piles flush to the wall. The lanes are empty. The lifeguard just now mounting his chair. You kick off your flip-flops and hurl yourself into the still, blue water. *First one in!*

FROM TIME TO TIME one of us will disappear for a week or two and aboveground inquiries are made. Emails are sent. Voice messages left. Old-fashioned notes are handwritten on thin, lined sheets of paper and folded up into neat quadrants and slipped under front doors. *Yoo-hoo, everything okay?* Usually it is nothing serious. A flare-up of tendonitis in the shoulder ("My dog's a tugger"). Jury duty. The annual mandatory company retreat. An out-of-town visitor who refuses to leave. Or maybe, like Alice, you simply forgot. But every so often the news is not good: *He defected.* Sometimes a swimmer will receive an unexpected ultimatum from an unhappy spouse above ground: *It's me or the pool.* Or they'll wake up one morning after twenty-five years unable to bear the thought of taking one more stroke. *It suddenly all seemed so pointless.* And that's that, we'll never hear from them again. But to all of those who have left us—willingly, unwillingly, or under duress—we just want to say: you can come back anytime and slip back into your old lane. We won't ask you any questions ("Where *were* you?"). We won't hold your absence against you. We promise to greet you warmly, but respectfully, and with a minimum of fuss. "Nice to see you again," we'll say, or "Been a while." But keep in mind that the second time you leave us, there is no coming back.

ONCE A YEAR, in mid-August, the pool is closed for ten days for maintenance and repairs and we do our best to reconnect with our neglected family and friends on land. We go out for drinks after work with our colleagues, we call our mothers, we do brunch, we do lunch, we take long postprandial strolls through the park. We try to catch up on all the things we've been putting off for months: renewing that driver's license, scheduling the colonoscopy, dusting, mopping, regrouting the bathroom tiles. Many of us, for the sake of marital harmony, use this time to take an extended aboveground vacation with our mates. But the minute we return home—before opening up our mail, before unpacking our suitcases, before airing out the house and wandering from one room to the next in a jet-lagged daze, apologizing to our wilted flowers and desperately watering our dying plants—we are out the door like a shot. *I've got to swim my laps.* Alice always forgets that the pool has been closed and every afternoon at two she can be seen knocking on the door of the aboveground entrance, but the building is dark, the doors are all locked, and she is wondering if the world has come to an end. *"Hello? Hello? Hello?"*

COTTON BALLS, wedding rings, one-half of a set of false teeth, two retainers, \$42.58 in loose change, three euros (recent visitors), four German marks (visitors from long ago), one Patek Philippe watch (still ticking) with expandable wristband, one wooden mousetrap (*sans* mouse), one yellow rubber duck (deflated), one pair of buffalo-horn glasses with the right lens (trifocal) slightly cracked—these are some of the things that have drifted down to the bottom of our pool over the years. Where their owners are today we cannot say for sure. Perhaps they have left the neighborhood and are swimming in foreign and, some would say, superior bodies of water: the Aegean, Lake Geneva, Montego Bay, the underground pool in Paris at the Hotel Ritz (*It's more like bobbing and preening than swimming*). Perhaps they are sunbathing on the Riviera. Perhaps they are still swimming here among us, oblivious to their loss. Perhaps they are you. If so, grab your ID card and climb up the two flights of stairs to the Lost and Found on Lower Level III. All found items will be held in our retrieval system (large blue plastic bin in the back of the storage closet) for two weeks before either being disposed of or donated to charity, or entering into the possession of the Aquatics Commissioner's brother, Stu. If you are lucky enough to find what it is you were looking for, do not pump your fist up and down in the air and shout out, "Yes!" A simple "Thank you" to the

Lost and Found attendant will do. If you find yourself plain out of luck, ignore the pang in your heart and tell the attendant, quietly, with a shrug, "Hey, it's just stuff." And whatever you do, do not ask for Stu.

THERE ARE THOSE who would call our devotion to the pool excessive, if not pathological. *I'm sorry about your compulsion to swim exactly sixty-eight laps.* Too many hours spent down below, our critics tell us, is a diversion, a distraction, a dereliction of our duties on land, not to mention unhealthy. We are reminded of the dangers of swimmer's ear, pinkeye, waterborne microbes, shallow-water blackout, the irreparable damage the chlorine does to our hair. *It feels like straw.* Is it really necessary, we are asked, to do the same thing, at the same time, every day, week after week, year after year, without fail? What about walking? What about sunshine? What about picnics? Birds? Trees? What, our exasperated friends and family members sometimes ask us, about *me*? And then they begin to enumerate our flaws: our fundamentally solitary natures, our craving for order, our intense desire, at the exclusion of all else, to be alone in the water with nothing but our own thoughts, our obsession with counting, as though the number of laps swum—our *yardage*—was somehow the true measure of our worth, our secret disdain for those who choose to reside permanently up above ("You think we're all *sofa people*"), our belief that a day has not been properly lived unless we've been down below, in the lanes, our inability to tolerate even the slightest deviation from our routine (*But I'll miss my swim!*), our aversion to chaos and spontaneity, indeed, to life itself. *You're no fun.* Loosen up, we are told. Skip a day. Skip two days. Swim sixty-seven laps instead of sixty-eight. Or did we want to spend the rest of our lives paddling back and forth inside a giant concrete box?

THE ANSWER, of course, is yes. Because for us, swimming is more than a pastime, it is our passion, our solace, our addiction of choice, the one thing we look forward to more than anything else. *It's the only time I feel truly alive.* It keeps us centered and focused, it slows down the aging process, it lowers our blood pressure, it improves our stamina, our memory, our lung capacity, our general outlook on life itself. Were it not for the pool, in fact, we'd probably all be dead. And so to our detractors—and to all of those who claim that it's "just endorphins"—we say come down, try it out, be our guest for a day. Grab a towel, put on your suit and cap, and walk over to the edge of the underground pool. Now adjust your goggles, extend your arms in front of you, one hand over the other, thumbs crossed, chin tucked to your chest, and take the rapturous plunge. You'll see. Once you get into the water you'll never want to get out.

WE KNOW, of course, that we cannot stay down here forever. Spouses sicken and need our round-the-clock care. *I can't leave her side.* Jobs are lost. Mortgage payments missed. Medications cease to work. T cell counts plummet. Alibis unravel. Planes go down. The biopsy report comes back positive. There's a shadow on your X-ray that wasn't there before. You slip on the no-slip mat getting out of the bathtub and you shatter your left knee. You go into the hospital for a routine cosmetic procedure and you never come out. You ignore the mole. You forget to change the battery in the smoke detector. You fail—*just this once*—to look both ways before crossing the street. You wake up one day and you can't even remember your own name (It's *Alice*). But until that day comes you keep your eyes focused on that painted black line on the bottom of your lane and you do what you must: you swim on. Your pace is steady but unhurried. *No need to rush.* Your form, good enough. Your mood is calm. You are back in your element again. *Just one more lap,* you tell yourself, *and I'm done.*

THE CRACK

At first it is barely visible, a faint dark line just south of the drain in the deep end of lane four. It flits briefly into view as you swim over it and then, once it has passed out of your field of vision, is instantly forgotten, like a dream that vanishes upon waking. If you blink, or are angling your head upward, toward the light, as you are surfacing for air, or are simply admiring the superior physique of the swimmer in the next lane, you will miss it. Many of us, older and no longer eagle-eyed, blind without our glasses, do not see the crack at all. Or if we do, we mistake it for something else: a piece of string, a length of wire, a scratch on the outer lens of our goggles. One of us, as she does almost everything, mistakes it for her own self. "I thought I had a floater in my eye!" she says. And for those of us slower swimmers who spend most of our time—most of our lives, it often seems—drifting and bobbing in the shallow end of the pool, the crack is nothing more than a rumor, news from a distant lane, to which we pay no mind.

ONE OF US, however, gets out of the water the moment he sees the crack and leaves without saying a word. "Dental appointment," someone says. Someone else says, "Spooked." Whatever the cause of his abrupt departure, we have not heard a word from him since.

FOR SEVERAL DAYS we eye the crack warily and wait for something to happen. For it to grow wider, or darker, or change in appearance and shape, or replicate itself, virus-like, in lanes seven and eight. But the crack remains stubbornly, silently, ineffably itself: a tiny hairline fracture no longer than a child's forearm on the bottom of our pool.

A FEW OF US believe it is bad luck to swim over the crack and begin avoiding lane four at all costs. "I think I'll do some drills," we say, and then we grab a kickboard and casually saunter down to lane one or two. Others of us in neighboring lanes three and five are curious about the crack and pass up no opportunity to sneak in a furtive sideways glance every chance we get. One of us, an off-the-books event planner in her life above ground with a brisk, no-nonsense stroke, says that she is determined to ignore the crack—"I refuse to let it have the upper hand"—but still finds herself staring at it every time she swims over it, practically against her own will. "I just feel compelled." Another of us swears that the last time he swam over the crack he felt a faint but insistent downward tug—"It was like flying over the Bermuda Triangle"—while others of us barely give it a second thought. Alice forgets about the crack the moment she gets out of the water and whenever somebody mentions it to her in the locker room she looks at them as though they were crazy. "Crack?" she says. "There's no crack."

THERE ARE THOSE of us, however, who are unable to suppress our alarm. What if the crack is a symptom of some deep-rooted systemic decay? Or a geological anomaly? Or the manifestation of a larger underground fault line that has been growing stealthily beneath us for years? Others scoff. The crack, they say, is purely cosmetic. A rust stain left behind by a wayward bobby pin that fell out of Alice's hair. *She doesn't always remember to put on her swim cap.* Or maybe, someone says, it's fake. Or a work of art. Or both: a masterpiece of trompe l'oeil. *All you'd need is a straight edge and a fine-point Sharpie.* Someone else suggests that the crack is not a crack at all but a wound that will eventually close up and heal, leaving behind only the faintest trace of a scar. For now, however, it just needs to breathe. "Give it some time," we are told.

FINALLY, THE LIFEGUARD is called over to settle the matter once and for all. He peers down hard into the clear blue water, silver whistle dangling from the knotted black shoestring tied around his neck, and then he shakes his head. "It's nothing," he says.

STILL, MANY OF US remain anxious. Because the truth is, we don't know what it is. Or what it means. Or if it has any meaning at all. Maybe the crack is just a crack, nothing more, nothing less. *A little bit of spackle might just do the trick.* Or maybe it's a rupture. A chasm. A miniature Mariana Trench. A tiny tear in the fabric of our world that no amount of goodwill can fix. None of us, of course, will dive down and touch it. "I'm afraid," someone says. Someone says, "I think I'm going to be sick." Someone says, "I wish I'd never seen it. Nothing will ever be the same again." All of us have questions: Is the crack brief or enduring? Banal or profound? Malignant or benign or—ethicist James in lane two—morally neutral? Where did it come from? How deep is it? Is there anything in there? Who is to blame for it? Can we reverse it? And, most importantly, *Why us?*

"WE'RE LOOKING INTO IT," the Aquatics Director tells us. The one thing he can say for sure is that the crack is not a leak. The water pressure remains steady. The level of the pool has not dropped. No seepage has been detected in the surrounding ground soil and the foundation remains sound and intact. Inspectors will be arriving on the scene shortly to evaluate the crack and track down its source and further updates will be made available as the situation unfolds. "These things happen," we are told. The crack is most likely a transient phenomenon brought about by the recent warming trends in the weather and by the end of the summer, pool officials predict, it will have played itself out.

AS FOR WHICH one of us saw the crack first—this question has been fiercely debated. Some say it had to be Vincent, the former drug dealer in lane five who is alert to his environment in ways the rest of us are not. *You'd think he'd read the bottom of the pool the way he reads a block.* But Vincent insists that the moment he gets into the water he "turns it all off." All he sees is that little black line running down the center of his lane. Nothing else. Others claim that "technically" it might have been Alice, who notices everything, as if for the first time ("There's a towel on your head!" she may say to you in the locker room), and then promptly forgets. Although we wonder: Can you be said to have seen something if you can't remember what it was you just saw? Still others argue that what matters most is not who saw the crack first, but that the crack has been seen. Perhaps the crack has been there all along, just waiting to make itself known to us.

ABOVE GROUND WE go about our lives as usual—we count out our pills, we go to our meetings, we shop, we eat, we placate our colleagues (*What I'm hearing you say is . . .*), we follow the protocol, we peer into our screens—but nothing feels quite real. *I'm thinking about it all the time.* Even those of us who claim to be unaffected by the crack are occasionally plagued by the nagging sense that something's amiss, only we can't remember what it is. Did we forget to back up our files? Lock in our mortgage? Turn off the stove? Apply liberal coatings of sunblock at regular two-hour intervals to every exposed surface of our hands, arms and face? Or we'll be talking to our spouses and see their mouths moving, but they suddenly seem a million miles away. "What's wrong?" they'll say to us. Or "Honey?" Or "Earth to Alice!" And then an image will briefly float into view—a faint wavering line—and for a moment we'll have no idea what day it is, or who we are talking to, or why, and then we'll shake our heads and, just as quickly as it appeared, the image will float away—*lost it*—and we are returned to our everyday lives. "I don't know," we'll say. Or "Everything." Or "I think I'm losing my mind."

SEVERAL OF US worry that the crack might somehow be our own fault. We feel ashamed of it, as though it were a blemish, a defect, an indelible flaw, a moral stain upon our soul that we have brought upon ourselves. "We shouldn't have excluded the children from the pool," someone says. Someone says, "We should have been nicer to that last lifeguard." "Payback," says another, "for our secret campaign to get rid of the synchronized swimmers the summer before last." (Although, one of us points out, they *deserved* it: "A bunch of show-offs.") "And did we really have to blame management," someone asks, "for every little thing that went wrong?" "And raise such a ruckus," asks someone else, "about that last raise in our annual dues?" "This is what we get," someone says, "for doing nothing but complain, complain, complain." "And deferring maintenance," someone else says, "for three out of the last four years." "I wish . . ." Alice says, and then her voice trails off. "Oh never mind what I wish." Someone else says, "Bad juju all around."

TEN DAYS AFTER the crack's initial appearance and inspectors admit they "still don't know what the heck it is." Although similar unexplained cracks have been reported in other pools across the United States and even in countries as far away as Japan (Tokyo, Hotel Okura, indoor lap pool, lane three: polite crack), Dubai (Bab Al Shams Desert Resort and Spa, infinity pool, "Jacuzzi spot": five-star crack) and France (Paris, Piscine Pontoise, wall-floor seam beneath the ladder: *fissure française*), none of them exactly resembles ours. "This thing is unprecedented," says Brendan Patel, professor of structural engineering at the polytechnic across town. US Geological Survey scientist Christine Wilcox says it's possible that the crack is the result of an underground microtremor too weak to be detected by local seismic monitors, which show no unusual ground activity in the area in the past thirty days. But then again, she adds, maybe not. We are assured, however, that the crack poses no immediate threat to our health or well-being and that the water is safe. "But whether or not we'll be able to get to the bottom of this," says Aquatics Task Force Advisor Carol LeClerc, "remains to be seen."

LONGTIME MORNING REGULAR Eleanor quietly empties out her locker and says she won't be coming back. "I think I'll sign up for a yoga class," she says. Aqua jogger Michael announces that he, too, is leaving the pool, "until the experts figure this thing out," and for the next three days Alice is not her usual, cheery self. "Where's Mike?" she keeps asking. But the rest of us swim boldly, bravely on. Although we wonder: Is there something that Mike and Eleanor know about that we lap counters, we lane plowers, we resolute refusers of sunlight and fresh air (*Who needs it?*), do not?

WHAT WE KNOW about the crack so far: it is not the result of a malfunctioning hydrostatic relief valve (Ted Huber, Certified Pool Inspector, ABC Pool & Spa: "Valve's good") or illegal after-hours drilling at a nearby construction site (Al Domenico, Project Manager, Integrity Construction: "Wasn't us"). It's definitely not a calamity (Pool Spokesperson Isabel Grabow: "This is definitely not a calamity") or a hoax (Safety Risk Officer Larry Fulmer: "It's real, people"), though there's a teeny tiny chance (Office of Structures mathematician Edison Yee: "We're talking statistically insignificant at best") that it's a mistake. *Oops, wrong pool.* Although the crack appears to be essentially docile in nature and bears us no apparent ill will, its true intentions remain bafflingly unknown. The inspectors will continue to investigate every possible natural and man-made cause and in the meantime pool officials are inviting any qualified experts with an even remotely plausible explanation to come forward at once.

ONE BY ONE, we drop our suggestions into the suggestion box on the Aquatics Director's door. Jonathan in lane three: "It's a superficial scratch." Water walker Francesca: "Idiopathic in origin." The disowned casino heiress in lane four with the double-jointed knees: "A stigmata?" Former high school swim coach and All-State swimmer Pastor Eileen: "Feeble cousin to the painted black line." George One: "It's an insult." George Two: "It's a joke." George Three: "It's a wake-up call, big time." The new guy in lane six with the navel ring and the yin-yang tattoo: "It's our own private San Andreas." Medical claims adjuster and devoted lane five swimmer Geraldine: "Not our problem. It's a preexisting condition that didn't happen on our watch." Our resident catastrophist and most elegant backstroker, Marv: "It's a sign from on high that our time below is up." The last of us to weigh in is retired circuit court judge Elizabeth, who scribbles down two words on the back of her most recent unpaid parking ticket and drops it into the Aquatics Director's box: *Inside job.*

OTHER EXPLANATIONS FOR the crack to emerge from the aboveground community at large include migrating soil conditions, defective Chinese concrete, a coming sinkhole, desperate plea for attention, act of God, something in the deep geology and—local astrologer Sahara—"a rare and unfortunate alignment of the planets in a particularly malevolent manner." Astronomy professor Nate Zimmerman is quick to call out Sahara's "so-called parade of planets" as "a big ole bunch of hooey." "Where's the science here?" he asks. There is also the expanding earth theory ("Do we need further proof that our planet is bursting at the seams?" asks Ace Hardware store owner Bob Esposito), the cosmic joke theory (*Ha ha ha ha ha ha ha ha ha*), the conspiracy theory (Rotary Club Treasurer Rick Halloran: "The Saudis did it") and the vibrations-from-heavy-truck-traffic-on-the-freeway theory (also known as the "big rig" or "too much rumbling" theory). None of these conjectures, however persuasive, has proved conclusive. "We're grasping at straws here," says Environmental Health and Water Quality Supervisor Theresa Boyd.

MOST MADDENING OF ALL, perhaps, is the mass psychogenic illness theory put forth by a small but vocal minority of aboveground nonswimmers (the crack deniers) who claim, without ever having once come down to the pool, that the crack is a purely "delusional" or "self-generated" phenomenon—a *folie à deux*—and if we'd all just pull ourselves together and stop thinking about it every second of the night and day, it would simply go away. The problem with this theory, however, is that once you've seen the crack, or *think* you've seen the crack, it quietly lodges itself, unbeknownst to you, in the recesses of your mind. And every time you swim over it, or even hear it mentioned secondhand ("Did somebody say it was *contagious?*"), it etches itself more deeply into the neural pathways of your brain. And before you know it, it's with you all the time. "It's the first thing I think about when I wake up in the morning," someone says, "and the last thing I think about at night before I go to sleep." Someone else says, "Actually, I'm obsessed." "What I want to know," someone says, "is what, if anything, will emerge from its depths?"

WE ARE HEARTENED, however, by the results of the most recent study, which indicate that cracks such as ours—tentative, barely there, scarcely visible to the naked eye, in a word, shy—tend to be indolent rather than aggressive in nature and spread at a nearly glacial pace. "These guys can hang around doing absolutely nothing for *years*," says chief engineer Henry Mulvaney of board-approved geotechnical engineering firm Mulvaney & Fried. Whereas a "true" crack, if left unattended for even a few hours, can easily run rampant and overwhelm an entire pool overnight. "We see this all the time." His final assessment: our crack is more of a pre-crack than a true crack per se. "Nothing to worry about," we are told. But independent investigator and forensic failure expert Professor Anastasia Heerdt warns us against taking "feel-good" engineer Hank Mulvaney's assessment too much to heart. "He's just telling you what you want to hear," she says. Her advice to us? "Get in your laps while you can."

"I DON'T LIKE THIS," says the normally fearless Gary in lane four. Sheila in lane seven admits that lately the only thing she can think about when she dives into the water is "When can I get out?" Sidestroker Dennis says he *is* getting out as—one, two, three—he nimbly hoists his hefty bulk back up onto the deck. "Enough's enough." Walter in lane three confesses that he never really liked swimming "all that much"—news to us ("Doctor's orders," he explains)—and won't be returning anytime soon, "if ever." ("That guy was just *looking* for an excuse not to swim," says lane mate Vivian.) Ruth in lane six says that although she's loathe to admit it—"It just feels traitorous"—she's thinking of trying out another pool. Alice says, "But there *is* no other pool." Saul says, "True. True." Afternoon regular Randall (gold chain, pull buoy, Mondrian print suit) is overheard in the men's locker room saying that he's "tired of the whole pool scene" and the next day he, too, is gone. But the rest of us swim stubbornly on.

AS THE DAYS pass by without further incident—no new cracks appear and the existing crack, "our" crack, does not budge so much as a fraction of an inch—our spirits begin to lighten and our anxiety slowly lifts. For it occurs to us that the crack might not be that bad after all. *If you just think of it as a line, it's not so scary.* Several of us, embarrassed by our initial displays of fear, now gamely swim over the crack every chance we get. Lane four avoiders sheepishly return. Former doomsdayers who were predicting mayhem and gloom—*This is the beginning of the end*—admit that they might have been overreacting or even—it does happen—just plain wrong. And those of us who once vigilantly monitored the crack every time we came down to the pool no longer find ourselves performing our ritual pre- and postswim "checks." *I forgot!* And for the first time in weeks we are calm.

"YOU CAN LEARN to live with anything," we tell ourselves. And "Everything happens for a reason." And—Rabbi Abramcik in lane three—"This is but a minor misfortune in a long string of continuous woes." Mrs. Fong in lane four just shrugs and says, "Been through worse." And a few of us—cheerful brightsiders through and through—profess to feel genuine gratitude for the crack's sudden and unexpected intrusion into our otherwise predictable belowground lives. *Stroke, stroke, breathe, stroke, stroke, breathe.* "Who knows?" says positive thinker Glenn in lane seven. "Maybe it'll be good for us, teach us a lesson." We feel enlivened by the crack, exhilarated by it, even, as though we'd been singled out for a special fate. "This doesn't just happen to *anyone*, you know," someone says. Someone else says, "It does add an element of surprise." Alice says, "It *is* a surprise." Someone says, "I feel like it's the thing I've been waiting for all my life."

ALTHOUGH IN OUR darker moments, we cannot help but wonder: *Is it a blessing in disguise, or is it just a disguise?* And if it's just a disguise, then what is it disguising?

THEORIES, OF COURSE, abound. Some say that the crack was deliberately planted by management as an excuse to shut down the pool. *It's all part of the plan.* And the lifeguard, these same people insist, is "in on it." *So be careful what you say.* Others have heard that the crack opens up onto a second and deeper world that lies just beneath the surface of ours. An alternate and perhaps truer world with its own underground pool filled with faster, more attractive people in less-stretched-out suits who nail their flip turns every time. "Like the masters swimmers, only better," someone says. "And nicer," says someone else. Someone else says, "They're our ideal us!" There is also talk of bottomless crevices, long-buried chemical waste sites, a collapsed salt mine, a subterranean river whose waters have flowed unimpeded for more than ten thousand years ("There are fish down there with no *eyes*") and a vast and vapid emptiness so great that to contemplate it for even more than a few moments would cause your mind to implode. *It's like we've been swimming over a void.*

BY THE MIDDLE of summer the novelty of the crack has begun to wear off and our attention slowly turns to other things: the installation of the new energy-saving showerheads in the locker rooms, the case of Provost Annette's missing Swedish goggles (still unsolved), an alleged groping incident in lane three (alleged groper whisked out of the building by security in five minutes flat), a fistfight in lane seven ("He refused to let me pass!"), Angelita's new psychedelic rainbow-swirls swimsuit, vintage circa 1969 (poolwide consensus: *It's a hit!*), the soul-scorching heat wave above ground—falling reservoirs, parched gardens, panting little dogs—that shows no sign of ever letting up. Some days we barely manage to give the crack a second thought, although it continues to surface unexpectedly in our nocturnal lives on dry land. *Last night I dreamed I had a splinter in my eye.* But most of the time it is simply there in the background, a faint but indelible razor-thin presence on the periphery of our world. So accustomed, in fact, have we become to the crack, that after a while we cease to see it at all.

AND SO WHEN, one day, we realize that, while we weren't looking, the crack has disappeared, we have to ask ourselves: Had we grown too comfortable with it? Did we come to take it too much for granted? Was it even really there? (Maybe we really *did* just imagine it?) "I could have *sworn* I saw it there this morning," says devoted lane four swimmer Leonard. And although many of us are relieved that the crack is now gone—"It was starting to get on my nerves," says sidestroker Shannon—a few of us already miss it, and harbor secret hopes for its timely return. We feel sadly diminished without it, as though a part of us had died. "It just made me feel really good to look at it every morning before I went in to work," someone says. Someone else says, "Every time I swam over it, I felt a quiet thrill." Alice swims her laps as usual but when she gets out of the pool, she doesn't have her usual postswim glow. "Something's wrong," she says. And those of us slow-lane swimmers in lanes one and two who kept meaning to stroll over and give the crack a good hard look now regret our dallying ways. "I just figured it would always be there," someone says. Someone else says, "*Now* I'm scared."

THE BIG QUESTION, for many of us, is where did it go? Into hibernation? Remission? Or did it just feel like taking the day off? Was it something we said? ("This thing is overrated." "A total time suck." "Too much talk of the town.") Or did? ("Let's just ignore it and see if it goes away.") Or could it have—apropos of nothing—spontaneously regressed? What are the chances of a same-lane recurrence? One in two? Two in three? Nada? Nichts? Zilch? Is it possible that the crack is still with us, only some unique alteration in its makeup has caused it to become undetectable to even the most discerning of human eyes? Or could it still be lurking, sleeper-cell-like, just beneath the surface, taking a quick breather before it reawakens and comes roaring back to life? Or did it simply grow tired of us and decide to move on to some other, better, more desirable body of water? The black-bottom pool in the Wellivers' backyard, perhaps (swim-up bar)? Or the two-story atrium fountain in the Asian food court at the mall (*pennies!*). Or, worse yet, did it just tire of being itself? "*Suicide,*" someone says. Someone else says, "Erased."

THE FOLLOWING MORNING, just as suddenly as it vanished, the crack reappears and, much to our surprise, many of us breathe a sigh of relief. *Life just wasn't the same without it.* According to assistant pool manager Maureen Engel, the crack was temporarily "cloaked" by an experimental "wet patch" that was applied to its surface by engineers sometime late Sunday night, but after an initial and promising period of rigid adherence—"Things were looking so good"—the patch failed to take. *Lost its stick.* And although many of us are glad to have the old crack back, something about it seems different. *It's just a little off.* Several of us are convinced that the crack has widened, ever so slightly, along its southern end, while others feel just as strongly that it's narrowed instead. *It's like it's winking.* Some say it seems "smoother" than before. Or frailer. Or a tad more beaten down. *It's lost some steam.* Others feel certain that it's bulked up, just a bit. One of us says that she detects a suspicious change in its contour—a slight sine-like curve—along the length of its western flank. *I think it's aged.* Another swears that the crack has migrated north, about a quarter of an inch, as though all along all it ever wanted was to be closer to the drain. Someone else suggests that maybe it *did* go down the drain, but didn't like what it saw (*Too much hair!*) and made a U-turn and came right back up. And a few of us suspect it's not even the same crack as before, but a malevolent and anarchic doppelgänger—a crack impostor—that has returned in its stead to take us all down in a whirling gyre of plastic flippers and doom. *We've got to stop this thing in its tracks.*

THE AQUATICS DIRECTOR urges all to "take ten" and get a grip, lest we lose ourselves in a "cacophony of conjecture." The crack, he tells us, has not been altered or enhanced in any meaningful way and any changes we may detect in its appearance are solely due to minute errors in our own perception. *If you stare at anything for long enough, you begin to see things that aren't there.* But when a second "sister" or "clone" crack—same length, same width, same color and hue—surfaces two days later at the bottom of lane five we cannot help but wonder if this is just a harmless local iteration—a copycat crack—or the beginning of something much worse. "It's the other shoe!" says Vicky in lane seven. Alice says, "What?" And shortly after lunch, when the new crack unexpectedly strikes out on its own, surging down the lane before putting on the brakes and coming to an abrupt halt mere inches from the wall ("contact inhibition," we are later told), even the most complacent of us—staid Steve—has to admit that "this can't be good." And the following evening, when two more small cracks are discovered hiding out on the border between lanes five and six—multiple primaries, we ask ourselves, or duplicate knockoffs of crack one?—we begin to suspect that our pool might be the site of a "crack cluster." "Or at least," says water walker Meg, "an unusually large visitation." Richard says, "This is an outbreak." Dana says, "Scourge." "The only word that comes to mind at this moment," says lane three breaststroker Mark, "is 'Help.'"

SHOULDN'T WE BE doing something? we wonder. Clapping our hands? Stomping our feet? Lighting a candle? Signing a petition? Calling the mayor? The police chief? The Director of Emergency Preparedness himself? *Hello, Floyd?* Or are we losing ground, asks patent attorney Liane in lane two, by hesitation? "You *know* those guys never answer their phones." "Could the authorities be misrepresenting the data?" asks sidestroker Sydney. "And those 'experts,'" says new member Alex, "do they even really exist?" ("And for that matter," asks metaphysician Gwen, "do *we*?") "It *is* kind of strange," says lane four freestyler Seung-ha, "that the engineers only do their work at night." Alice says, "Let us all just try and have a good time."

FOUR CRACKS, one pool is, the inspectors inform us, "more of a sprawl situation than a cluster." "Grossly unremarkable." "Below the threshold of suspicion." "A statistical aberration within the normal range of chance." *Pure fluke.* But when, the following week, three more cracks appear in rapid succession in the middle of lanes six and seven, noted stress analyst Dr. Denise Kovats of the Structural Hazards Countermeasures Division admits that "there might be something going on." And by the time our first "vertical crack" is discovered, late one afternoon, just before closing, near the bottom of the wall at the shallow end of lane two, inspectors say the odds are less than one in 6.3 million that the cluster is a purely random event. In fact, they say, they're pretty sure it's here "on purpose." Still, they maintain, it is manageable. "We're monitoring this thing round the clock." No water loss has been detected, no structural deficiencies have been found and no immediate action, for the time being, is required. "We're on top of it."

THE NEXT DAY the lanes are emptier than usual, the showers less steamy, the locker rooms not quite so loud. "I don't want to say I'm afraid," says thirty-year veteran Tim, "but I'm in a low-grade panic all the time." Charlotte in lane six says, "There is something horribly wrong with this earth." Normally unflappable backstroker Felice says she's thinking of tossing in an extra Mass this week, "just in case." "Just in case what?" asks Alice. Sidestroker Audrey says she's heard, off the record, from a reputable source close to pool management, someone who is briefed daily, if not hourly (the Aquatics Director's wife's best friend, Pam), that the cluster is actually "much worse than they're letting on." *The pool could fail at any time.* Someone else says he's heard, from an equally reputable source whose identity, for reasons of discretion, he prefers not to disclose ("Let's just call her 'X'"), that the cluster has been artificially "staged" for our own personal terror and delight. "It's a test," he says. There are also whispers of bungled permits, botched repairs, fabricated inspection certificates, ignored summonses, sleepy examiners, overcaffeinated hydrologists, underpaid auditors, a slightly too friendly visit from a well-dressed lobbyist ("Cherie") for the Chlorine Institute and somewhere, up high, in a tiny airless room many floors above us, a trio of drunken statisticians endlessly tossing out numbers until late in the night. *Let's just call the upper threshold . . . five!*

FOR ONE MONTH the cluster neither expands nor contracts but remains as is, harmlessly hovering in a classic "holding pattern," which Cynthia Greeley, chief environmental degradation expert at the Institute for Geology and Geophysics, predicts could be remarkably durable in length. "Time's on your side." But no sooner have we lulled ourselves into believing that the cluster may have finally run its course—*It's over!*—than several new cracks begin to surface in the deep end of the pool. Some of them are thicker than their predecessors, with darker middles and less uniform edges, while others look strangely bloated (although of course, we remind ourselves, they *are* underwater). And a few of them—a quartet of cracks quietly flourishing in the shadow of the diving board in the middle of lane six ("Our cluster has a cluster," says wise guy Stan)—appear ragged and unkempt, mildly deranged, some might even say insane. We are still, however, "a long ways from squiggly." And although many of us suspect that we are in the presence of a heartier and more aggressive "second-generation" crack with an infinite capacity to dominate and thrive, experts tell us that, appearances to the contrary—"Do not be fooled by the illusion of vitality," warns water shapes failure engineer Clifford Hwang—these newest fractures are unusually inert and are not expected to cause us any harm during the normal lifetime of the pool.

IN OUR REAL LIVES, on dry land, we are more preoccupied than usual. We misplace our keys. We forget to pay our bills. We can't remember our passwords. We neglect to comb our hair. We are late to the office. We can't concentrate on our work. In the middle of conversation, we sometimes stand up and wander off. *I have to check my stocks.* Our performance reviews suffer. Our likability ratings decline. Our friends begin to avoid us. Our partners accuse us—rightly—of being distracted and self-absorbed. "Is there somebody else?" they ask us. Or they order us to "stop moping" and get out of the house. *Swim it off!* And at three o'clock in the morning, as they lie beside us peacefully slumbering away, we wake up in a cold sweat, cheeks flushed, teeth clenched, hearts pounding, wondering: How many more laps do we have left? One hundred? One thousand? Six? Ninety-four? Isn't there somebody out there who can give us a clue?

FIRST IT IS announced that the annual August closure will be extended from ten days to two weeks so the pool can be drained and the crack situation properly assessed. And we breathe a sigh of relief. *They've got this thing under control.* Then it is announced that the pool will be closed for three weeks instead of two so the broken underwater speakers can be replaced and additional repair work performed. And we think, *Okay, okay, it's just a minor sprucing up.* (But also, somewhere in the back of our minds: *What* underwater speakers?) Then it is announced that the pool will not reopen until the first of September so the lane lines can be repainted and new suction entrapment technology installed. And we have to ask ourselves: *Is there something we're not being told?* Finally a small handwritten notice is posted, early one morning, on the bulletin board beneath the clock, informing us that the results of the investigation will be announced at an emergency "town hall" meeting in the bleachers the following afternoon at a quarter past two. Attendance, though not mandatory, is "strongly suggested" for all users of the pool.

". . . BUT AFTER RULING out every humanly imaginable theory," the Aquatics Director concludes, "the inspectors have determined that the cluster's cause may never be found." "Our very best guess?" says lead investigator Karen Lubofsky. And then she shakes her head. "We've run out of guesses." Subterranean structures specialist and Public Security Board Advisor Chris Mendoza urges us to "accept the mystery" and move on. "Because there are some things in this world," he explains, "that just can't be explained." "Basically," the Aquatics Director tells us, "we're stumped." The cluster could disappear tomorrow, or continue to spread insidiously, beneath the surface, with growth zones extending eastward toward the post office and southwest along the upper edge of the De Lorenzos' well-manicured front lawn, or grow so slowly that it would never cause us any harm. But since there is no way of predicting with any certainty which one of these paths a cluster of unknown etiology will take, out of an abundance of caution pool officials have decided to assume the very worst—progressive and possibly exponential expansion leading to eventual catastrophic collapse. "And so, for the safety of swimmers and staff alike, effective as of three p.m. on the last Sunday in August the pool will be permanently closed. Thank you," the Aquatics Commissioner tells us, "and goodbye." And just like that, our number is up.

"THIS IS A NIGHTMARE," someone says. "A disaster," says someone else. Linda climbs up to the top row of the bleachers and silently begins to weep. "But I thought," Rose says, "that we could stay down here forever." The other Rose says, "Maybe we have?" Normally rule-abiding Clarence dives down into the water without removing the Band-Aid from his left knee and when he surfaces two lengths later says, "I wish I'd never learned how to swim." Even the lifeguard looks slightly taken aback. "Lost his job," someone says. Slow-lane Thaddeus, eighty-nine tomorrow and still swimming strong, smiles sadly into the air as he inserts his earplugs into his ears for the ten thousandth time. "It all went by so fast," he says. Lane mate Murray says, "Where's my meds?" Lane two sidestroker Irene quietly snaps the seat of her swimsuit and stares down at her feet. "But I was so happy in my lane," she says. Alice says, "Me too."

OTHERS OF US, however, feel strangely relieved. The terrible thing we have been waiting for has finally happened. A weight has been lifted. A shadow has passed. The uncertainty is over. This is it. The end. *No more fun for us.* And now we can move on.

UP ABOVE, LIFE goes on as always. Children screaming in the park, young people sitting in cafés, drinking black coffee and smiling blandly into their phones, patiently attended old men, eyes ever on the horizon, grimly pushing their green-tennis-balled walkers inch by inch down the shady side of the street. *Coming through!* Whenever we run into someone we know we feel anxious and exposed, as though we were carrying a shameful secret, but nobody seems to notice that anything's wrong. "Hello, stranger!" they'll say, or "How's it going?" And suddenly we find ourselves discussing the new parking garage, the price of real estate, our latest redecorating dilemma in the home, but it all feels vaguely quaint and pretend.

AUGUST BEGINS LIKE a slow, shattering dream. Heat rises up from the dusty sidewalks. Lawns bake. Trees droop. The flowers have all lost their smell. A lone Good Humor truck, illegally double-parked near the entrance to the school playground, drones its slow maniacal song. But down below, at the pool, we throw ourselves into the cool, clear blue water and we carry on. Breaststroker Enid placidly swims her laps as usual, with her head held high, as though she had not a care in the world. *Pull, kick, glide, pull, kick, glide.* Aqua jogger Jim runs like crazy for five minutes and then pauses, for a moment, to admire his shrinking gut. "Hey, man, look at that." Claude loses an earring. Donald stubs a toe. Suzette is nearly sideswiped by a careless fellow swimmer in her lane but for once she does not succumb to her rage. *Let it go.*

WE ARE KINDER now, more yielding. In a word, less uptight. *The new niceness,* we call it. Boundaries loosen up. Intralane rivalries dissolve. Grudges are forgiven. *So what if she once unplugged my hair dryer in the locker room?* Pretenses fall away. Formerly reckless passers once intent on getting ahead at all costs now proceed with the requisite tap on the foot just like everyone else. "It's not always about winning," says second-fastest freestyler Bruce. Ankle yankers desist. Tailgaters cease to tail. Lane bullies rein it in. Fast- and slow-lane swimmers who never had much to say to one another now exchange pleasantries, postswim, as they are toweling off on the deck. "Where'd you get that cap?" Even the hitherto remote former Olympian breaks her silence and dispenses the occasional free tip: "You need to soften up that right leg!" Because we are all equals now in the face of our common end.

THIS IS THE NEW REALITY, we tell ourselves. And, *We're gonna get through this.* And—dogged paddler Lilian in lane three—*God works in all things for the good.* But then a moment later, we'll think, *My life is wrecked.* Or we'll climb up out of the pool before we've finished our last lap because what's the point of going on when all you've got left is just a couple of weeks? "All that counting and kicking, and for what?" asks the normally sanguine Kate in lane seven. Water jogger Trudy unfastens the buckle on her flotation belt and says, "The thrill is gone." But the rest of us swim determinedly on.

EVERY NOW AND THEN one of us will bump into an early defector above ground—in the dairy aisle at Vons, coming out of the barbershop, while standing in line at the Au Delice Bakery waiting for a freshly baked loaf of artisanal country bread—and their message for us is always the same: *It's not so bad.* Twenty-year veteran Howard (weak upper body, powerfully explosive kick), who up and left us the day the first crack appeared, says that, with the exception of pulling out of the market right before the last crash, getting out of the pool was the best decision he ever made in his life. "All I was doing was going round in circles." Former lane four freestyler Anika (short yellow flippers, tense, inefficient stroke), who left us three days after Howard, says that instead of going swimming three times a week she now does tai chi every morning at dawn with all the old Chinese people in the park. "I've never felt so serene." Flawless backstroker Leslie (lap counter, nose clamp, hypermobile limbs) says that three weeks after leaving the pool she forgot she was ever there. "It's like it never happened." Former lane hog Brian (three years, five collisions, four of which were his fault) just shrugs and says, "Honestly? I never looked back. *No regrets.*"

SEVERAL OF US begin making brief forays into alternate aboveground bodies of water, "just to see." *A trial run.* Clara buys a day pass at the Peninsular Hotel, but reports back that the pool there is so small that by the time you dive in and take three strokes, it's time to turn around. Janet tries braving the unruly waters at the public pool downtown ("It's positively antediluvian in the lanes!"). Jason goes to the beach ("Too salty"). Brenda dips a hesitant toe into the community pool at the municipal Y ("It's like a bathtub!"). Barbara uses her free guest pass at Omega Fitness, which has an eight-lane lap pool identical in length and width to ours, but says, "It's just not the same" (*potted palms, chaises longues*). Only one of us—Charles, who is at this very moment slicing through the water like the competitive high school swimmer he once was (captain of the swim team, Northwood Senior High)—has found a suitable alternate arrangement in his life above ground: the rooftop pool at his new boyfriend Eliot's condo at the corner of Ocean and Fourth (*potted palms, chaises longues!*).

UNTIL THE VERY last week a few of us continue to hold out hope that we might somehow be saved. "Surely," says morning regular Hugh, "there must be *somebody* up there who can intervene on our behalf." "The Aquatics Director's wife," someone says. "Or Pam!" says someone else. Ella says, "Maybe we'll be granted an extension." "Or a reprieve," says lane three backstroker Daniel. "I'd be happy with a little blessing," says lane buddy Patrick, "just to know that somebody up there cares." "Nobody up there *cares,*" says insurance actuary Fran. Others of us begin making our own private bargains. *If I swim sixty-four laps in under twenty-eight minutes then we'll be given an extra month. If I don't have a drink for three days in a row then they won't close the place down at all.* And several of us—stubborn refuseniks through and through—think, simply, No. This can't be happening to us. Because isn't this the sort of thing that usually happens to *other* pools? Weren't we supposed to be—hadn't they always told us we were, hadn't they *promised*—special? Different? Immune? *Exempt?* Or is it, simply—newly minted Buddhist "Ryojo" (Josh to us) in lane six—"just fate"? Or, simpler yet—pediatric oncologist Min-hee in lane seven—a case of plain dumb bad luck? Empty nester Yolanda pushes her goggles up, aviator style, onto her forehead, and says, "Everything is loss."

THE EXCEPTIONAL RESPONDERS among us insist that the closure might not necessarily be such a bad thing. "This is just the beginning," they tell us. And, "It's an opportunity to stop shuffling around in our flip-flops and finally go up there and start living life 'for real.'" *No more quick dips into the water whenever the going gets tough.* We'll fall in love with our spouses again (*the stranger you married*). Push past our comfort zones. Volunteer at the homeless shelter. Ask for a raise. Write a "gratitude" letter (*Thanks, Mom!*). Improve our balance. Our posture. Our attitude toward life itself. *No more complaining for me!* We'll open up our own business. *John's Consulting.* Finish writing that second novel. Start a journal. Throw a dinner party. Have an epiphany. Become a "people person." Get to know our neighbors. *Wanna borrow a cup of sugar?* Remember, for once, to look up at the sky. Because there's more to life than just following that little black line.

AS THE SUMMER drifts ever closer to its inevitable end we grow more and more resigned to our fate. *It's all over.* People linger for an extra moment or two before getting out of the pool even though they know, full well—*No idling, postswim, in the lanes!*—that they are breaking the rules. "What are they going to do, kick us out?" asks Marlene. Roger forgoes his obligatory preswim shower. Dorothy fails to put on her cap. Ian gives the Staff Only door an extra-hard push just because "it's something I've always wanted to do." (Nothing happens.) Eric scrawls his initials across the red hand on the Larceny Alert poster in the stairwell just because, Why not? Lane rival Esteban follows suit. *I was here too!* Belinda nods to the lifeguard and the lifeguard—a first ("Did you *see* that?")—nods back. Kevin gathers up the courage to speak to fellow lane three swimmer Abigail, with whom he has been secretly in love for more than ten years. "Nice goggles," he says. And Abigail, who yearns for the distant Daria in lane eight (*Way out of my league*), just smiles and says, graciously, "Thanks." Everett suggests that we all have a reunion. And Herschel, a picnic in the park, even though we're not exactly the picnicking sort. "Can't stand 'em," says Jennifer. Nolan says he doesn't mind "picnics *per se*" but is deathly allergic to bees. "And anyway," says Emily, "do we really want to see each other in our clothes?" Alice says, "Of course!"

SOMETIMES, IN THE middle of the night, we lie awake trying to imagine the pool without us. The lifeguard's empty chair standing tall by the bleachers. The scoreless scoreboard. The sharp chlorinated tang of the uninhaled thick wet air. The long-poled skimmer net propped up in the corner, secretly dreaming of better things—a dead leaf, a butterfly, a crocodile, a little brown bird, something, anything, besides the usual haul of rubber bands and tangled-up knots of hair. The two diving boards securely bolted down to the deep end, twangless and quiver-free. The yellow lane buoys their naturally buoyant after-hours selves. *Let's party!* The slightly sagging ropes. *We're so tired.* The soft purr of the recently serviced electric pump. *Ommm . . .* The frantic hands of the pace clock whirling ceaselessly, mindlessly forward through the dark. The flat glassy surface of the water itself, a serene blue rectangle floating over the wrecked floor of our world. And then we'll close our eyes and drift off into sleep and in the morning, when we wake, for one blissful moment we forget that in five days, in three days, in two days, *tomorrow*—our world is about to come to an end. And then we'll see it—a filament, a flicker, a brief flash on the very edge of our retinas that barely registers as a linear event. And try though as we might to return to the safety of sleep it's too late. The sun is streaming in through the curtains, the alarm clock is ringing, the garbage truck is banging and wheezing down the wrong side of the street. We're up.

THE LIFEGUARD BLOWS his whistle—three shrill tweets followed by one long sustained blast—and then shouts out the two familiar words: "Everybody out!"

ONE OF US takes off her goggles and squints up at the clock just to make sure that it's really time (it is). One of us strokes over to the ladder in the corner and says, "Now why'd he have to do *that*?" Two of us cry out, "No!" One of us clings to the tiled edge of the pool, panting and out of breath. "My heart is broken," she says. Another of us can't find his glasses. "Did you ever have the nagging feeling," someone else asks, "that you've just wasted your entire life?" Several of us can't speak. Many of us—most of us—are not even here. Either we don't swim on the weekends or we do, but earlier, in the morning, before the midday crush. Several of us would normally be here at three o'clock on a Sunday afternoon, but at the last minute something more pressing came up: a sick parent, a monster migraine, a not-to-be-missed open house. "I think this is *the one*." One of us is a self-professed unsentimental person who "doesn't do" goodbye. Another of us has been out with a torn rotator cuff for two weeks but made a special point to come down to the pool because she knows this is where she truly belongs. "Up there I'm just passing as me." One of us is here but really wishes he were not. "Already, this feels like the past." One of us is still at brunch. One of us continues to swim back and forth in her lane long after everyone else has gotten out, and when we call out her name—"Alice, time's up!"—the lifeguard lifts his hand and says, quietly, "One more lap."

AND WHEN SHE'S swum her last lap she takes a long hot shower in the locker room and changes back into her clothes and then climbs up the stairs and emerges, blinking and stunned, into the bright, blazing world above.

DIEM PERDIDI

She remembers her name. She remembers the name of the president. She remembers the name of the president's dog. She remembers what town she lives in. And on which street. And in which house. *The one with the big olive tree where the road takes a turn.* She remembers what year it is. She remembers the season. She remembers the day on which you were born. She remembers the daughter who was born before you—*She had your father's nose, that was the first thing I noticed about her*—but she does not remember that daughter's name. She remembers the name of the man she did not marry—Frank—and she keeps his letters in a drawer by her bed. She remembers that you once had a husband, but she refuses to remember your ex-husband's name. *That man,* she calls him.

SHE DOES NOT remember how she got the bruises on her arms or going for a walk with you earlier this morning. She does not remember bending over, during that walk, and plucking a flower from a neighbor's front yard and slipping it into her hair. *Maybe your father will kiss me now.* She does not remember what she ate for dinner last night, or when she last took her medicine. She does not remember to drink enough water. She does not remember to comb her hair.

SHE REMEMBERS THE rows of dried persimmons that once hung from the eaves of her mother's house in Berkeley. *They were the most beautiful shade of orange.* She remembers that your father loves peaches. She remembers that every Sunday morning, at ten, he takes her for a drive down to the sea in the brown car. She remembers that every evening, right before the eight-o'clock news, he sets out two fortune cookies on a paper plate and announces to her that they are having a party. She remembers that on Mondays he comes home from the college at four, and if he is even five minutes late she goes out to the gate and begins to wait for him. She remembers which bedroom is hers and which is his. She remembers that the bedroom that is now hers was once yours. She remembers that it wasn't always like this.

SHE REMEMBERS THE first line of the song "How High the Moon." She remembers the Pledge of Allegiance. She remembers her Social Security number. She remembers her best friend Jean's telephone number even though Jean has been dead for six years. She remembers that Margaret is dead. She remembers that Betty is dead. She remembers that Grace has stopped calling. She remembers that her own mother died four years ago, while watching the birds out the window, and she misses her more and more every day. *It doesn't go away.* She remembers the number assigned to her family by the government right after the start of the war. *13611.* She remembers being sent away to the desert with her mother and brother during the fifth month of that war and taking her first ride on a train. She remembers the day they came home. *September 9, 1945.* She remembers the sound of the wind hissing through the sagebrush. She remembers the scorpions and red ants. She remembers the taste of dust.

WHENEVER YOU STOP by to see her she remembers to give you a big hug, and you are always surprised at her strength. She remembers to give you a kiss every time you leave. She remembers to tell you, at the end of every phone call, that the FBI will check up on you again soon. She remembers to ask you if you would like her to iron your blouse for you before you go out on a date. She remembers to smooth down your skirt. *Don't give it all away*. She remembers to brush aside a wayward strand of your hair. She does not remember eating lunch with you twenty minutes ago and suggests that you go out to Marie Callender's for sandwiches and pie. She does not remember that she herself once used to make the most beautiful pies with perfectly fluted crusts. She does not remember how to iron your blouse for you or when she began to forget. *Something's changed*. She does not remember what she is supposed to do next.

SHE REMEMBERS THAT the daughter who was born before you lived for half an hour and then died. *She looked perfect from the outside*. She remembers her mother telling her, more than once, *Don't you ever let anyone see you cry*. She remembers giving you your first bath on your third day in the world. She remembers that you were a very fat baby. She remembers that your first word was "No." She remembers picking apples in a field with Frank many years ago in the rain. *It was the best day of my life.* She remembers that the first time she met him she was so nervous she forgot her own address. She remembers wearing too much lipstick. She remembers not sleeping for days.

WHEN YOU DRIVE past the swim club, she remembers being kicked out of the pool by the lifeguard after swimming in that pool for more than thirty-five years. *I couldn't remember any of the rules.* She remembers doing ten arm swings on the deck before diving down into the water. She remembers not needing to take a breath for almost the entire first length. She does not remember how to use the "new" coffeemaker, which is now three years old, because it was bought after she began to forget. She does not remember asking your father, ten minutes ago, if today is Sunday, or if it is time to go for her ride. She does not remember where she last put her sweater or how long she has been sitting in her chair. She does not always remember how to get out of that chair, and so you gently push down on the footrest and offer her your hand, which she does not always remember to take. *Go away,* she sometimes says. Other times, she just says, *I'm stuck.* She does not remember saying to you, the other night, right after your father left the room, *He loves me more than I love him.* She does not remember saying to you, a moment later, *I can hardly wait until he comes back.*

SHE REMEMBERS THAT when your father was courting her he was always on time. She remembers thinking that he had a nice smile. *He still does.* She remembers that when they first met he was engaged to another woman. She remembers that that other woman was white. She remembers that that other woman's parents did not want their daughter to marry a man who looked just like the gardener. She remembers that the winters were colder back then, and that there were days on which you actually had to put on a coat and scarf. She remembers her mother bowing her head every morning at the altar and offering the ancestors a bowl of hot rice. She remembers the smell of incense and pickled cabbage in the kitchen. She remembers that her father always wore very nice shoes. She remembers that the night the FBI came for him he and her mother had just had another big fight. She remembers not seeing him again until after the end of the war.

SHE DOES NOT always remember to trim her toenails, and when you soak her feet in the bucket of warm water she closes her eyes and leans back in her chair and reaches out for your hand. *Don't give up on me,* she says. She does not remember how to tie her shoelaces, or fasten the hooks on her bra. She does not remember that she has been wearing her favorite blue blouse for five days in a row. She does not remember your age. *Just wait till you have children of your own,* she says to you, even though you are now too old to do so.

SHE REMEMBERS THAT after the first girl was born and then died, she sat in the yard for days, just staring at the roses by the pond. *I didn't know what else to do.* She remembers that when you were born you, too, had your father's long nose. *It was as if I'd given birth to the same girl twice.* She remembers that you are a Taurus. She remembers that your birthstone is green.

She remembers to read you your horoscope from the newspaper whenever you come over to see her. *Someone you were once very close to may soon reappear in your life.* She does not remember reading you that same horoscope five minutes ago or going to the doctor with you last week after you discovered the bump on the back of her head. *I think I fell.* She does not remember telling the doctor that you are no longer married, or giving him your number and asking him to please call. She does not remember leaning over and whispering to you, the moment he stepped out of the room, *I think he'll do.*

SHE REMEMBERS ANOTHER doctor asking her, fifty years ago, minutes after the first girl was born and then died, if she wanted to donate the baby's body to science. *He said she had a very unusual heart.* She remembers being in labor for thirty-two hours. She remembers being too tired to think. *So I told him yes.* She remembers driving home from the hospital in the sky blue Chevy with your father and neither one of them saying a word. She remembers knowing she'd made a big mistake. She does not remember what happened to the baby's body and worries that it might be stuck in a jar. She does not remember why they didn't just bury her. *I wish she were under a tree.* She remembers wanting to bring her flowers every day.

SHE REMEMBERS THAT even as a young girl you said you did not want to have children. She remembers that you hated wearing dresses. She remembers that you never played with dolls. She remembers that the first time you bled you were thirteen years old and wearing bright yellow pants. She remembers that your childhood dog was named Shiro. She remembers that you once had a cat named Gasoline. She remembers that you had two turtles named Turtle. She remembers that the first time she and your father took you to Japan to meet his family you were eighteen months old and just beginning to speak. She remembers leaving you with his mother in the tiny silkworm village high up in the mountains while she and your father traveled across the island for ten days. *I worried about you the whole time.* She remembers that when they came back you did not know who she was and that for many days afterwards you would not talk to her, you would only whisper in her ear.

SHE REMEMBERS THAT the year you turned five you refused to leave the house without tapping the doorframe three times. She remembers that you had a habit of clicking your teeth repeatedly, which drove her up the wall. She remembers that you could not stand it when different-colored foods were touching on the plate. *Everything had to be in its place.* She remembers trying to teach you to read before you were ready. She remembers taking you to Newberry's to pick out patterns and fabric and teaching you how to sew. She remembers that every night, after dinner, you would sit down next to her at the kitchen table and hand her the bobby pins one by one as she set the curlers in her hair. She remembers that this was her favorite part of the day. *I wanted to be with you all the time.*

SHE REMEMBERS THAT you were conceived on the first try. She remembers that your brother was conceived on the first try. She remembers that your other brother was conceived on the second try. *We must not have been paying attention.* She remembers that a palm reader once told her she would never be able to bear children because her uterus was tipped the wrong way. She remembers that a blind fortune-teller once told her she had been a man in her past life, and that Frank had been her sister. She remembers that everything she remembers is not necessarily true. She remembers the horse-drawn garbage carts on Ashby, her first pair of crepe-soled shoes, scattered flowers by the side of the road. She remembers that the sound of Frank's voice always made her feel calmer. She remembers that every time they parted he turned around and watched her walk away. She remembers that the first time he asked her to marry him she told him she wasn't ready. She remembers that the second time she said she wanted to wait until she was finished with school. She remembers walking along the water with him one warm summer evening on the boardwalk and being so happy she could not remember her own name. She remembers not knowing that it wouldn't be like this with any of the others. She remembers thinking she had all the time in the world.

SHE DOES NOT remember the names of the flowers she planted with you three days ago in the garden. *Roses? Daffodils? Immortelles?* She does not remember that today is Sunday, and she has already gone for her ride. She does not remember to call you, even though she always says that she will. She remembers how to play "Clair de lune" on the piano. She remembers how to play "Chopsticks" and scales. She remembers not to talk to telemarketers when they call on the telephone. *We're not interested.* She remembers her grammar. *Just between you and me.* She remembers her manners. She remembers to say thank you and please. She remembers to wipe herself every time she uses the toilet. She remembers to flush. She remembers to turn her wedding ring around whenever she pulls on her silk stockings. She remembers to reapply her lipstick every time she leaves the house. She remembers to put on her antiwrinkle cream every night before climbing into bed. *It works while you sleep!* In the morning, when she wakes, she remembers her dreams. *I was walking through a forest. I was swimming in a river. I was looking for Frank in a city I did not know and no one would tell me where he was.*

ON HALLOWEEN EVE, she remembers to ask you if you are going out trick-or-treating. She remembers that your father hates pumpkin. *It's all he ate in Japan during the war.* She remembers listening to him pray, every night, when they first got married, that he would be the one to die first. She remembers playing marbles on a dirt floor in the desert with her brother and listening to the couple at night on the other side of the wall. *They were at it all the time.* She remembers the box of chocolates you brought back for her after your honeymoon in Paris. "But will it last?" you asked her. She remembers her own mother telling her, "The moment you fall in love with someone, you are lost."

SHE REMEMBERS THAT when her father came back after the war he and her mother fought even more than they had before. She remembers that he would spend entire days shopping for shoes in San Francisco while her mother scrubbed other people's floors. She remembers that some nights he would walk around the block three times before coming into the house. She remembers that one night he did not come in at all. She remembers that when your own husband left you, six years ago, you had just published your first book. She remembers thinking he was trouble the moment she met him. *A mother knows.* She remembers keeping that thought to herself. *I had to let you make your own mistakes.* She remembers that you broke out in hives all over your body for weeks.

~~~~~~
~~~~~~

SHE REMEMBERS THAT, of her three children, you were the most delightful to be with. She remembers that your younger brother was so quiet she sometimes forgot he was there. *He was like a dream.* She remembers that her own brother refused to carry anything with him onto the train except for his transistor radio. *He didn't want to miss any of his favorite shows.* She remembers her mother burying all the silver in the yard the night before they left. She remembers her fifth-grade teacher, Mr. Martello, asking her to stand up in front of the class so everyone could tell her goodbye. She remembers being given a silver heart pendant by her next-door neighbor, Elaine Crowley, who promised to write but never did. She remembers losing that pendant on the train and being so angry she wanted to cry. *It was my first piece of jewelry.*

SHE REMEMBERS THAT one month after Frank joined the Air Force he suddenly stopped writing her letters. She remembers worrying that he'd been shot down over Korea or taken hostage by guerrilla fighters in the mountains. She remembers thinking about him every single minute of the day. *I thought I was losing my mind.* She remembers learning from a friend one night that he had fallen in love with somebody else. She remembers asking your father the next day to marry her. *"Shall we go get the ring?" I said to him.* She remembers telling him, *It's time.*

WHEN YOU TAKE her to Ralphs she remembers that coffee is aisle two. She remembers that aisle three is milk. She remembers the name of the cashier in the express lane who always gives her a big hug. *Diane.* She remembers the name of the girl at the flower stand who always gives her a single broken-stemmed rose. She remembers that the man behind the meat counter is Big Lou. "Well, hello, gorgeous," he says to her. She does not remember where her purse is, and begins to grow frantic until you remind her that she has left it at home. *I don't feel like myself without it.* She does not remember asking the man in line behind her whether or not he was married. She does not remember him telling her, rudely, that he was not. She does not remember staring at the old woman in the wheelchair by the melons and whispering to you, *I hope I never end up like that.* She remembers that the huge mimosa tree that once stood next to the cart corral in the parking lot is no longer there. *Nothing stays the same*. She remembers that she was once a very good swimmer. She remembers failing her last driver's test three times in a row. She remembers that the day after her father left them her mother sprinkled little piles of salt in the corner of every room to purify the house. She remembers that they never spoke of him again.

SHE DOES NOT remember asking your father, when he comes home from the pharmacy, what took him so long, or who he talked to, or whether or not the pharmacist was pretty. She does not always remember his name. She remembers graduating from high school with high honors in Latin. She remembers how to say "I came, I saw, I conquered." *Veni, vidi, vici*. She remembers how to say "I have lost the day." *Diem perdidi*. She remembers the words for "I'm sorry" in Japanese, which you have not heard her utter in years. She remembers the words for "rice" and "toilet." She remembers the words for "wait." *Chotto matte kudasai*. She remembers that if you dream of a white snake it will bring you good luck. She remembers that it is bad luck to pick up a dropped comb. She remembers that you should never run to a funeral. She remembers that you shout the truth down into a well.

SHE REMEMBERS GOING to work, like her mother, for the rich white ladies up in the hills. She remembers Mrs. Tindall, who insisted on eating lunch with her every day in the kitchen instead of just leaving her alone. She remembers Mrs. Edward deVries, who fired her after one day. *"Who taught you how to iron?" she asked me.* She remembers that Mrs. Cavanaugh would not let her go home on Saturdays until she had baked an apple pie. She remembers Mrs. Cavanaugh's husband, Arthur, who liked to put his hand on her knee. She remembers that he sometimes gave her money. She remembers that she never refused. She remembers once stealing a silver candlestick from a cupboard but she cannot remember whose it was. She remembers that they never missed it. She remembers using the same napkin for three days in a row. She remembers that today is Sunday, which six days out of seven is not true.

WHEN YOU BRING home the man you hope will become your next husband, she remembers to take his jacket. She remembers to offer him coffee. She remembers to offer him cake. She remembers to thank him for the roses. *So you like her?* she asks him.

She remembers to ask him his name. *She's my first-born, you know*. She remembers, five minutes later, that she has already forgotten his name, and asks him again what it is. *That's my brother's name*, she tells him. She does not remember talking to her brother on the phone earlier that morning or going for a walk with you in the park. She does not remember how to make coffee. She does not remember how to serve cake.

SHE REMEMBERS SITTING next to her brother many years ago on a train to the desert and fighting about who got to lie down on the seat. She remembers hot white sand, the wind on the water, someone's voice telling her, *Hush, it's all right*. She remembers where she was the day the men landed on the moon. She remembers the day they learned that Japan had lost the war. *It was the only time I ever saw my mother cry*. She remembers the day she learned that Frank had married somebody else. *I read about it in the paper*. She remembers the letter she got from him not long after, asking if he could please see her. *He said he'd made a mistake*. She remembers meeting him one last time and telling him, afterwards, "It's too late." She remembers marrying your father on an unusually warm day in December. She remembers having their first fight, three months later, in March. *I threw a chair.* She remembers that he comes home from the college every Monday at four. She remembers that she is forgetting. She remembers less and less every day.

WHEN YOU ASK her your name, she does not remember what it is. *Ask your father, he'll know.* She does not remember the name of the president. She does not remember the name of the president's dog. She does not remember the season. She does not remember the day or the year. She remembers the little house on San Luis Avenue that she first lived in with your father. She remembers her mother leaning over the bed she once shared with her brother and kissing the two of them good night. She remembers that as soon as the first girl was born she knew that something was wrong. *She didn't cry.* She remembers holding the baby in her arms and watching her go to sleep for the first and last time in her life. She remembers that they never buried her. She remembers that they did not give her a name. She remembers that the baby had perfect fingernails and a very unusual heart. She remembers that she had your father's long nose. She remembers knowing at once that she was his. She remembers beginning to bleed two days later when she came home from the hospital. She remembers your father catching her in the bathroom as she began to fall. She remembers a desert sky at sunset. *It was the most beautiful shade of orange.* She remembers scorpions and red ants. She remembers the taste of dust. She remembers once loving someone more than anyone else. She remembers giving birth to the same girl twice. She remembers that today is Sunday, and it is time to go for her ride, and so she picks up her purse and puts on her lipstick and goes out to wait for your father in the car.

BELAVISTA

You are here today because you have failed the test. Maybe you were unable to draw all the numbers on the clock face, or spell "world" backwards, or remember even one of the five unrelated words that were just recited to you, mere minutes ago, by one of our professionally trained testers. Or maybe, for the first time ever, you just couldn't copy that cube. "I'm not in the mood," you said. Or perhaps your name-the-animal skills have atrophied since we last saw you. Or you totally botched the executive function alternating trail-making section. Or your social integration score came back as a dismal one. Or maybe you didn't even take the test. Maybe you went out to the supermarket to buy a carton of eggs and came back two days later with an overripe mango instead. "Got it!" Or you tried to race past a fire truck—"But I signaled!"—or couldn't remember how to make your famous rustic plum tart. Or perhaps, unbeknownst to you, you have become an *extremely difficult* person to live with. You won't eat. You won't bathe. You get up ten and sometimes twenty times a night, driving your loved ones to exhaustion. Or maybe your husband simply put you in the car this morning and told you he was "taking you for a ride." Or your daughter announced that she had "made arrangements" and you thought, *Great, a plan.* And here you are.

WELCOME TO BELAVISTA. We are a long-term, for-profit memory residence conveniently located on a former parking lot off the freeway just minutes from the Valley Plaza Mall. Other names we have gone by in the past include Heritage Pointe, Palomar Gardens, Municipal Ward #3 and The Villages at Pacifica, Inc. Also, the nice place, the new place, the last place, a *wonderful* place ("You'll *love* it") and, most recently, by an eight-year-old boy to his mother from behind the tinted-glass windows of a rapidly departing SUV, The Bughouse.

HERE AT BELAVISTA we will do everything we can to meet your evolving needs as you begin this next and final phase of your journey. Once you have been processed by our Enrollment Team (welcome reception, gift basket, full-body mole and sore check) you will be assigned a room, a number, a bed and, if you did not bring your own, a new set of clothing complete with easy iron-on identification tags. From now on, you will never have to worry about losing your way again. Because even if *you* don't know where you are, *we* know where you are. In the unlikely event that you happen to stray off the premises (travel outside your "safe radius"), your GPS wander guard will instantly inform us of your geographical coordinates on the grid. At night, your sleep will be remotely tracked by electronic sensors. If you attempt an unaccompanied exit from your bed your pressure-sensitive floor mat will activate the mobility alarm and a member of your Memory Team will arrive shortly to assist you.

BUT, YOU MAY be thinking, I don't have it (you have it). Or, I did great on the test (you did abysmally). Or, My husband is coming to pick me up tomorrow (he lied). Or, I have to catch the next bus into town (the bus stop is fake, the bus, nonexistent). Or, How did this happen? (Slowly, over decades or—Alan, Room 19, car-train collision while trying to beat the gate—quickly, in an instant.) Or, Really, I think I've had enough (sorry, but this is only the beginning).

A FEW FACTS about your condition. It is not temporary. It is progressive, intractable and irreversible. Ultimately, like life itself, it is terminal. The medication will not stop it. Green tea infused with gotu kola and ginkgo biloba will not stop it. Prayer will not stop it. Qigong, "working the steps" and "living more purposefully" (too late for that) will not stop it. Having an unrealistically positive attitude will not stop it and may, in fact, even hasten your decline. There are no exceptions to these rules. Although you are a special person, yours is not a special case. There are eighty-seven other people at Belavista and more than fifty million worldwide who are similarly afflicted.

WHO GETS IT? you may be wondering (as well as, Is this a joke? Am I under arrest? And, Did somebody just take my car keys?). Wealthy Mexican drug lords get it. Wildcat Chinese miners in Brazil get it. Unusually good-looking Ivy League professors in the movies get it. Seven-time nominees for the Nobel Prize in Chemistry in Leipzig, Germany, get it (Nobel Prize winners, however, do not, due to the salutary effects of the "winner's boost" on their immune systems). Geriatric prisoners at San Quentin serving out their last years under the three-strikes-and-you're-out drug laws get it. In a remote inbred fishing village on the northeast coast of Iceland, two out of three people above the age of fifty get it. In an even more remote village in the northern Andes consisting of several large extended families all descended from the same sixteenth-century Spanish conquistador, one in two people under the age of forty-five gets it. On an unnamed tropical island in the southwest Andaman Archipelago, nobody gets it (life span too short). And then, of course, there's you, the tiny cohort of one. You got it.

THERE IS NO "meaning" or "higher purpose" to your affliction. It is not a "gift" or a "test" or an opportunity for personal growth and transformation. It will not heal your angry, wounded soul or make you a kinder, more compassionate person who is less judgmental of others. It will not ennoble your paid carers ("She's a *saint*") or enrich the lives of those around you who have always loved and adored you. It will just make them sad. Nor will it bring you closer to the higher being or liberate you from your formerly petty concerns. If you worried about your weight before, you will worry about your weight now ("I'm *still* too fat," you will say). All it will do is bring you closer to your own inevitable end.

CANCER WOULD BE better, you may be thinking. Or heart disease. Or a bullet straight through to the brain. Or maybe you are simply filled with regret for all the things you did not do. You should have done more crossword puzzles, taken more risks, signed up for that Great Books class, used up all your vacation days, removed the plastic slipcovers from the "good" furniture ("I'm turning into my mother!" you once said, accurately), worn those expensive heels in the back of your closet you were saving for that special occasion (which would be *what?*). You should have *lived* (but what did you do instead? You played it safe and stayed in your lane). Or maybe you should have chosen the Mediterranean Diet over the Atkins. Or learned a new language—French, German, bahasa Indonesia, something, *anything*—before the age of fifty, when your brain began its inevitable downhill slide. "Next year," you kept saying to yourself. And now—*Surprise!*—next year is here. Now you will never take that trip to Paris or become a well-read person (instead of just a mere browser) or speak fluent or even passable French. *Nous sommes désolés.* Because the party, sadly, is over.

AS OUR NEWEST admission to Belavista, there are a few things you should know. You will wake when we decide you will wake. You will sleep when we put you down and turn off the lights. All seating in the Dining Room is assigned (if you require more than the allotted forty-two minutes to finish your food you may request a seat at one of our "slow eater tables"). Do not wander the halls late at night looking for your husband or children (your husband is sound asleep in the big empty bed, your children are grown and scattered across the globe). Do not try to open the windows (the windows do not open) or mindlessly punch random numbers into the coded lock by the elevator doors (the code is uncrackable). If you fail to remain compliant, we may have to give you a pill. If you resist your customized care plan, we may have to give you a pill. If you refuse to take your pill, we may have to give you a pill plus, depending on the degree of your intransigence, an injection. Hoarding is prohibited. Socks are imperative. The door to your room must remain open at all times. If you follow the rules and maintain a cheerful demeanor, you may be selected as our next "Resident of the Month."

IT DOES NOT matter who you were "before" in what you call your "real life" (remember, this *is* your real life). You could have been a bus driver (Norman, Room 23, got lost on the route he'd driven every day for the past thirty-eight years). Or a professor of English (Beverly, Room 41, could no longer follow her students' comments in class: *What's the difference between the signifier and the signified?*). Or the governor of a major state, the name of which now escapes you (William, Room 33: "Was it Maine?"). You could have been a medical biller (Vera, Room 17, bought her husband the same tie on sale at JCPenney's three days in a row: "Do you like it?" "I *love* it!"). Or a retired soap opera actress (Peggy, Room 27, wakes up every morning panicked that she has forgotten her lines). Or just a professionally ill person (Edith, Room 8, you name it, she's had it). Nobody knows and nobody cares.

Because the only thing that matters at Belavista is *who you are now.*

THE ACCOMMODATIONS AT Belavista, though modest, are comfortable and clean. Each of our semiprivate rooms comes fully furnished with two beds (height adjustable), two side tables (faux wood), two guest chairs (vinyl) and one privacy curtain (also vinyl). Your name and that of your roommate will be neatly printed on a single laminated card hung outside your door. The view from your window will consist of either a freeway underpass, the north end of the staff-only parking lot or the inglorious backside of our town. If you would like a larger room with abundant sunlight and a view of trees and grass, you will be charged extra (residents with nature views, studies strongly suggest, have less white matter shrinkage than residents in sunless rooms overlooking brick walls). If you would like access to one of our "top doctors" rather than a mere trainee, you will also be charged extra. If you cannot afford a top doctor but would like a "better" or "nicer" trainee with a more obliging bedside manner, you will still be charged extra, but not as much extra as you would be charged for a top doctor. Bimonthly visits from a volunteer dog therapy team provided by the Good Dog Foundation are charge-free.

IF YOU WERE expecting something different—high-thread-count sheets, custom furnishings, organic yogurt and granola for breakfast, fresh three-berry sorbet delivered to your room on demand—you should have gone to The Manor on the other side of town. Or just checked in to a hotel. All we can say is, we're sorry, we wish it were otherwise, once your husband has signed the Do Not Release order, however, there is nothing more we can do.

BUT THERE IS no way I can pay for this, you are probably thinking. Do not worry, your husband has already liquidated his retirement accounts, signed over to us your future Social Security payments and taken out a second mortgage on the house in order to finance your stay. That is, if you are one of our preferred-rate "private pay" residents. If, however, he made some bad investments over the years or has a long history of unpaid taxes or—Lloyd, Room 38—he fell for an online scam and blew through all his assets in one click ("But she *loved* me!"), then you are one of our "fixed-income" residents (a medically indigent person) and the government will reimburse us only a pittance for your stay. You still, however, do not need to worry. Contrary to popular belief, you will not be considered a second-class citizen or left to languish, for hours, unattended, in our "economy ward" (there is no economy ward). Even though we are losing money on your bed every day. Because here at Belavista we pride ourselves on treating each and every one of our residents with dignity and respect, regardless of their ability to pay.

WE DO, OF COURSE—off the record—have our favorites. Our ideal resident is well-groomed, attractive in appearance (easy on the eye) and, preferably, female. She is a native-born English speaker of pleasant disposition. Her appetite is robust—we are penalized by the state for every pound that you lose, thus our heavy reliance on carbs—though not gluttonous. Her hygiene is impeccable. She gets along well with her roommate and keeps her side of the curtain neat, tidy and free of crumbs. She does not rip off her name tag every five minutes ("I *know* who I am") or insist upon making funny noises alone in her bed after dark. She does not repeatedly ask, "Is there melon today?" or "Where's my daughter?" In fact, she does not ask any questions at all. She is docile and incurious, verging on meek. A "follower." Her family, if she has one, is too busy to properly oversee her care although they donate generously once a year.

HOW LONG WILL you be here? The short answer is, it depends. You could be here for several days, several years, a matter of hours or—Gordon, Room 3, PSEN4b gene carrier—more than half your lifetime. Ideally, you will be with us indefinitely. Realistically, however, you will not. Some leave us early for the hospital and never come back. Others slip away quietly, without warning, in the middle of the night. Most, however, remain with us patiently, peaceably, until their time is up.

ALTHOUGH THERE IS currently no treatment available to stop the progression of your disease, you can rest assured that the scientists are working 24/7 on your case. A cure, they say, will be available any day now. *We're starting the Phase III trials on Monday.* Or maybe they've already found a cure but it only works for people with a specific gene mutation on chromosome 17, which you, and 97.2 percent of the world's population, unfortunately, do not carry. Or maybe there is a cure but it only lasts for a few months, and only for a select few people in a cross-longitudinal study in the Netherlands ("The Rotterdam Study"), which no other lab, thus far, has been able to replicate. *The data points don't line up.* Or maybe there is no cure. Or maybe there is, but if you've missed the critical window for treatment it won't be effective. *Too late for you.* Rajesh ("Ray") Kapoor, Professor of Epidemiology and Developmental Neurobiology, Stanford University: "It's a tough nut to crack." Takashi Uematsu, Senior Investigator, the Center for Population Brain Health, University of Tokyo: "We are nearing the cusp of an inflection point." Ingemar Björkholm, Clinical Biochemist at the Karolinska Institutet: "Honestly? We still don't have a clue."

ON OCCASION YOU may hear a pleasantly disembodied voice floating out over the intercom and down through the halls. "Paging all supervisors! Paging all supervisors!" This is the voice of our Director, Nancy Lehmann-Hayes, PhD (a.k.a. "Dr. Nancy").

Dr. Nancy reports directly to corporate, a nondescript glass-clad building in a faraway tax-friendly state. She carries a monogrammed handbag and makes over $400,000 a year. Her main responsibility is to keep the shareholders happy. Her favorite word is "metrics." Her silent mantra is "A head in every bed." Her sole—and most precious—commodity is you. Dr. Nancy can be found in her office Monday through Thursday between the hours of ten a.m. and four p.m., poring over the latest financial reports. On her desk, facing outward, are two framed photographs of her three beautiful young children, frolicking in the sun. If you would like to schedule an appointment with Dr. Nancy, you must speak first with her Communications Officer, Melissa. Melissa, like everyone else who works here except for Juan, the maintenance man, is a woman. Melissa can be found Monday through Friday in the back of the client acquisition office, calling up her latest leads. *I would put my own mother here!* To speak to Melissa you must first place a request with her assistant, Brittany, who may or may not exist. Remember, Dr. Nancy is the public face of Belavista. Never make fun of Dr. Nancy. If you make fun of Dr. Nancy, you may become the subject of a Non-Compliance Report and our Behavioral Management Technologist will deal with you accordingly.

SOME ADVICE FOR your first day. Tell your husband, "Don't worry, I'll be fine," or "You tried," and then pick up your suitcase and follow your designated Greeter down the hall to your room without delay. Do not look back. Do not rush to the corridor window and wave frantically at the back of your husband's car as it slowly drives away (he can't see you). Do not ask if there is something you could have done differently (there is nothing) or who will explain your absence to the ladies in the locker room at the pool now that you are "away" (no one, they already know). Do not think, *Discarded*. Do not think, *Remaindered*. Do not think, *Culled from the herd*. Instead, put down your suitcase and introduce yourself to your new roommate. Open up your complimentary Amenities Kit (lip balm, Q-tips, extrasoft pair of nonskid rubber-soled socks). Pretend to understand.

AFTER LIVING IN a large three-bedroom house with your husband for more than forty years, you will now be sleeping four feet away from a complete stranger. She may be a retired schoolteacher. "Take one and pass it on, take one and pass it on." Or a former hotel manager always ready to lend a sympathetic ear. "I understand your frustration." She may be a thief. She may never stop talking. She may end up being the best friend you never had. If she keeps you up all night long grinding her teeth, insert your earplugs (see Amenities Kit). If she insists upon having complete control of the privacy curtain, suggest to her that you take turns. If she complains to her Memory Minder that you have "too many flowers," kindly give her some of yours. Do not embarrass her. Work toward compromise. Do your best to get along. Sit with her by the window in the Rec Room after Craft Time. Watch the clouds slowly scudding across the sky. Wait for nightfall. Try not to think about doors (all doors to the outside are double-dead-bolted and alarmed). Remember that she, too, is from someplace else.

PLEASE NOTE, A period of adjustment is normal. If, however, after one month you still cannot tolerate the thought of spending even another minute in your roommate's presence, you may place a "Request for

Transfer" (RFT) with the Bed Allocation Committee and someone will contact you when an appropriate opening becomes available (because at a place like Belavista, there is "churn"). You are allowed a maximum of three RFTs, after which you will be labeled nonadaptive, resistant to change or, worse yet, sent to the Refocus Room (don't ask).

THINGS FROM YOUR life before that you will have no use for at Belavista include: your expired Ralphs Rewards card (you will not be going grocery shopping again anytime soon), your oversized reinforced umbrella with the white clouds on the underside (nor will you soon be encountering "real weather"), your wedding ring (guaranteed to go missing within days), your quilted nylon jacket (indoor-living attire only, please, daytime temperatures at Belavista are a consistent seventy-two degrees all year round), your prized collection of useless bits of string (no comment) and your week At-a-Glance day planner (from now on, every day will be planned for you in advance). Stuffed animals are also discouraged (we are not a nursery), as well as any and all original artwork you may have created in the last five years. No photographs on the windowsills (windowsills are designated clutter-free zones). No mini fridges. No "outside" furniture. No crucifixes above the bed, please (we are an icon-free institution with a strict "no-thumbtack" policy).

FULL DISCLOSURE: not everything at Belavista is as it seems. The alarm clock bolted to the table beside your bed is a motion-activated surveillance camera. Your red see-through Sanicup is a hydration tracker. The thermostat below the light switch is a microphone. Your stylish silver ankle bracelet is a backup location device. The applesauce on your dinner plate is a medication-delivery vehicle. Ditto for the mashed potatoes and occasional big chunks of banana. The lovely carpet on your bathroom floor is an impact-reducing fall mat. Your "personal trainer" is a physical therapist. Her friendly greeting—"Looking good!"—a confidence amplifier. The gardener outside your window is a security guard. And that mildly baffled-looking woman staring back at you from the bathroom mirror? She is *you*.

WITH THE EXCEPTION of your doctor, who will visit you once a month for three minutes to sign off on your meds before closing your chart ("Nice to see you again") and hurrying out the door ("Next!"), you will be tended to exclusively by exhausted middle-aged women of color from cash-starved countries who work two and three jobs to cover the rent. Their blood pressure is high, their backs are sore, they haven't seen a dentist in years. Remember to thank them when they come to you in the middle of the night to fix your blanket. "Stay with me," you will say (Memory Minders must remain "on-task" at all times). Do not be offended if they don't have time to look up from their paperwork the next morning in the Day Room to greet you. *If it's not charted, it didn't happen.* Try to make their lives easier, if you can. They are being paid the lowest possible wage to love you.

THERE WILL BE—if you are lucky—entire days to get through. You may end up passing the time like Miriam, in Room 11, walking ceaselessly through the corridors for hours upon end. "Has anyone seen my hairbrush?" Or your gait may slow down to an uneven shuffle. Or you may decide to stand at the window every afternoon after lunch while your stomach begins to settle, watching the cars roll by (a favorite pastime of many of our male residents). "There's *no way* that guy is going to make the light." As a general rule, however, you can expect to spend approximately thirty-two percent of your free waking hours doing nothing, thirty-six percent of your free waking hours doing next to nothing and the remainder of your free time in moderated group activities such as Circle Time (optional but highly recommended), Purposeful Play (mandatory), Mind Your Mind Brain Games and both the free and tangible-prompt versions of Let's Reminisce. For an additional fee you can also enjoy the benefits of personalized music therapy (African bongos that imitate the beat of the human heart), blue-spectrum light therapy guaranteed to reset your circadian clock within minutes (this program is temporarily on hold until the facility-wide tunable LED installation project has been completed) and one-on-one brain boosting sessions with Neuro Coach Deb (a combination of hippocampal stim, Montessori-based category-sorting exercises and good old-fashioned memory flash cards, all custom-designed to help you momentarily rekindle your lost or diminishing, or—worst-case scenario—totally snuffed-out synaptic spark). Solitary self-soothing activities such as bead "work," placidly coloring between the lines and pretending to read in the Library also have a naturally calming and, some might say, even sedating effect and are strongly encouraged.

YOUR MAIN ACTIVITY, of course, will be waiting. For the medication to kick in. For "Afternoon Snack." French Fry Fridays. Your birthday (a single candle on a frosted cupcake at lunch). Your monthly appointment with Miss Sharon at our in-house beauty salon. "Just a trim, please," you will say. For the next phone call from your daughter ("I'm fine!" you will tell her). For any small act of kindness. A hand on your shoulder. A tap on your wrist. A hug. A squeeze. A wink. A nod. For someone to crouch down beside you and look you straight in the eye and say, "Everything's going to be all right" (to which the old you would reply, "You have *no idea* what you are talking about"). And last, but not least, for the sweet oblivion of sleep.

NIGHTS AT BELAVISTA begin promptly at eight, when the night-lights go on simultaneously in every room (you will never experience total darkness again) and the ambient temperature begins to drop. Evening med pass is at eight-thirty. Ten o'clock is lights-out. Room check is at eleven. Midnight rounds begin at one. If you find yourself lying wide awake at three in the morning, staring up at the thin strip of light on the ceiling (*What did I do wrong?*), you may want to "order in" from our "sleep menu," which offers a broad array of products designed to usher in a state of optimal rest (all items can be billed "a la carte" to your monthly invoice): vibrating eye masks, slow-wave headbands, thermo-sensitive "cool" hats, weighted fleece blankets guaranteed to create a swaddling sensation reminiscent of being in your first and very best bed, the womb. Graham crackers and juice, however, are not available (see our "no nocturnal comestibles" rule). Neither are boring bedtime stories, pulse point oils, affectionate snuggles and touches or, sadly, "husband pillows."

EVERY NOW AND THEN a well-meaning family member, friend or former colleague may appear, unbidden, in your doorway. "Knock knock!" This person is what is known as a Visitor. Visitors arrive clumped together, in droves (your "lady friends" from the pool). They trickle in singly, both before and after work (your friend Sylvia), and during their lunch breaks (your friend Marjorie), or in guilt-induced spasms (your daughter), on their way back home from the mall. "Hi, Mom!" They fly in once a year, from London (your older son) and New York (your younger son). They come bearing boxes of sugar-free cookies from the supermarket (your husband). Bouquets of tired white lilies from the same supermarket (the "good" florist was closed). Fresh sprigs of basil from your garden, which you will never see again. "Close your eyes and smell." They lean in close and ask, "Do you know who I am?" as though you were a complete idiot (you are *not* a complete idiot). They tell you about the weather ("Hot!"). The drive over ("Made good time!"). How great you look, even though you are listing ever so slightly to one side from your mid-morning meds. They ask you if we are treating you all right (the correct answer is Yes). They chat up the staff. They admire the flowers. They study the week's menus. They ask informed questions. "Is this *food?*" Often, they complain. Why is your blouse unbuttoned? Where are your glasses? And what is your favorite silk scarf doing wadded up in a dust-covered ball beneath your roommate's bed? After a while, though, they grow quiet. They glance at their watches. They check their phones. They stand up. They stretch.

And then, of course, they leave you. There are offices to get back to, emails to answer, rainforests to conserve, spin classes to attend. These people are *busy.* Busy. Busy. Busy! "I wish I could stay longer," they say. Or "Love you!" And you will find yourself quietly fuming. *Then don't go!* Though what you will say is "Please come see me again."

UNLESS IT IS QUIET HOUR (Thursday afternoons from three p.m. to four), the TV must remain on at all times. Even if you are not in your room, the TV must remain on. Even if you are in your room but the newscaster is speaking in an incomprehensible and, you suspect, possibly fictitious foreign tongue (*Plain English, please!* you may find yourself shouting at the screen), the TV must remain on. Even if you are able to understand what the newscaster is saying but the news—a school shooting in real time, a nuclear meltdown, an attack of killer bees, stonings and beheadings in a faraway oil-rich kingdom—is so upsetting that you want to put on your best dress and jump out the window, which, as we mentioned earlier, does not—and now you know why—open, the TV must remain on. Even if you are asleep, hallucinating, delirious, on the phone or—heaven forbid—catatonic, the TV must remain on (in the last case, of course, with the volume turned down low). Because the TV is not for your entertainment but for that of our staff. Wherever you are likely to find a staff member, you are more than likely to find a TV: in the Dining Room (next to the Have You Washed Your Hands? sign), in the physical therapy room (above the antigravity treadmill), in your bedroom (inches above your bed, on the end of an adjustable arm) and, of course, in the redundantly named TV Room (giant flat-screen mounted to the wall above the Purell dispenser), which, pending approval by corporate, will soon be renamed the Multi-Media Room (one computer, one TV, a wicker basket full of last month's magazines). Because every room at Belavista is, in a sense, the TV Room.

THE ONE EXCEPTION being the lobby. The lobby—leather lounge chairs, lavish floral arrangements, complimentary fruit bowl, tastefully framed photographs of dramatic black-and-white landscapes personally curated by Dr. Nancy herself—is a TV-free zone of silence and respect reserved for prospective residents and their families. The only audible sounds in the lobby are the fugitive murmurs of newly arrived guests checking in with the Lobby Ambassador at the concierge desk ("This place is *gorgeous*") and, in the background, the soothing plash of our shimmering Wall of Water. No residents in the lobby allowed.

OTHER AREAS THAT are off-limits to residents include the staff break room, the medication room, the vending alcove (residents are encouraged to adhere to their nutritional goals at all times), the back office, the front office, the Gift Shop, the Family Conference Room (everyone in your "outside" family is allowed at your team conference except for you) and anything on the other side of the UV-tinted glass (the green grass is for Visitors only).

A WORD ABOUT language. Here we say "where you are in the sequence," not "your condition is worsening." We say someone is "presymptomatic," not "But she seems totally normal!" And, "Let's pursue this to the next level," not "It's time to up your meds." Problems we would rather not deal with are referred to as "nonissues" and forwarded to the Care Quality Committee for "further study and consideration." Serious health code violations are "onetime mistakes." "Outside" people are "the unaffected." And a room with some windows punched into it is called "the Conservatory" (not to be confused with "the Day Room"). Platitudes we will never utter include "You'll get through this" and "Tomorrow is a better day" (we do not believe in compassionate deception). Nor will we ever refer to you as "Sweetie" or "Bed 37B" or "the Ivalo mutation carrier in Room 21." We will call you, simply, by your name.

OTHER THINGS WE will not do: We will not let you take the easy way out or turn your face, prematurely, toward the wall (you must "stay on the path" until the very end). We will not congratulate you for ordinary everyday accomplishments or speak to you in an unnaturally cheerful tone of voice. Rumors to the contrary, we will not give up on you. We will provide you with a stimulating but not overly demanding environment in which you can flourish and thrive. No more "masking" or fake nods of the head as you struggle to work your way through the name-face conundrum. *Abby. Betty. Clara?* No more mirroring. "How are you?" "How are *you?*" No more notes-to-self taped up all over the house. *Socks first,* then *shoes.* No more racking your brain for the right word when a good-enough word will do. *Can they tell?* (They can.) At Belavista you can say goodbye to those yellow Post-it notes and your bag of mnemonic tricks and, for the first time since the onset of your symptoms, you can let down your guard and feel at home among your own. Because here at Belavista, *everyone* knows.

LIKE MANY WHO suffer from afflictions similar to yours, you may develop a sudden and inexplicable love of trees. We do not know why this is. Even if you were not a "tree person" before, in your "old life," you may wake up one morning with a profound and novel appreciation of the sycamore standing outside your window (assuming, that is, that you are lucky enough to be in a room with a nature view). "Look at that," you may say, as though you had never really *looked* at anything before. Or maybe you were always a nature lover in theory who kept meaning to go for a hike—you were going to take the kids to Muir Woods!—but then you got old and never did. *I forgot!* And now here you are, sitting in your chair by the window, gazing out urgently, raptly at "your" tree—its shapely green canopy, its black velvety shadows, its sinuously curved trunk, its barky brown bark. "Look, *look*," you will say. "*See?*" You have fallen in love—*at last*—with a tree. As soon as you wake, every morning, you will pull aside the curtain and "check" to make sure that your tree is still there. And every morning, much to your joy and amazement, it will be. And every night, right before you go to bed, you will gaze out at its familiar yet mysterious silhouette one last time. *There it is!* You could spend your entire life looking at this tree, you think—and on some days, it may occur to you, you *have*—and that would be enough. Beauty apprehended. A life well lived. You will have glimpsed into the heart of the sublime.

IF, HOWEVER, YOU happen to be assigned to a room overlooking the back of the UPS Store, we are more than happy to install, for a not-insubstantial fee, one of our "virtual windows" with convincing long-view images of trees in the size and shape of your choice. Or, if you prefer something even more true to life, you may want to consider one of our most popular simulated greenspace options: "real-time trees" with enhanced depth illusion that "grow" at a "natural" rate. We can also "re-create" the backyard view from the home you have just left behind. *Don't forget the power line!* you may say. Or even, if you so desire, the view of your mother's persimmon tree from your childhood bedroom window. And if you cannot afford to go virtual, we are more than happy to dial up Dave's Lawn and Garden and order in a potted plant.

ONE OF THE low points of your year will be the much-dreaded Carol Week—the mandatory songfest decreed by management during which you will be sung at continuously, aggressively and, at times, contemptuously ("They're all *loonies*"), for eight, nine and ten hours a day. Blind accordion players will serenade you nonstop during your mealtimes. Dueling gospel choirs will compete for your ear in the corridors and urge you to join in the fun. Packs of tiny Cub Scouts will surround you in the Great Room, belting out *Jingle bell, jingle bell, jingle bell rock.* "Not *again.*" Our advice to you: sit back, relax and let the music in. Because nothing could make these people happier than to go home knowing they have made you their good work. And when the last caroler has exited the building and the racket finally comes to a stop, the usual din of Belavista will have never sounded so sweet: the pleasant pinging of the call bells, the exuberant ringing of the phones (*It's for you!*), the happy manic buzz of the overhead fluorescent lights, the strident yet friendly voice of Life Enrichment Manager Jessica over the intercom, announcing a birthday, an anniversary or simply that "Activities are now over and it is time for you to return to your room."

YOU MAY, AT TIMES—dusk, Sunday evening, the middle of winter—find yourself suddenly overwhelmed by an intense physical desire to go home. All you want to do, you tell yourself, is sit down in front of the TV with your husband on the ugly brown couch and eat cold leftover lo mein noodles one last time. And that would be enough. *Just one ordinary day.* And then, you tell yourself, you'd gladly come back (because, you will begin to realize, *this place really isn't that bad*). So you grab your purse and slippers and put on your lipstick and head for the emergency exit at the end of the hall. "Be right back, guys," you say, casually, to your Memory Team, as though you were just stepping out of the lab at the hospital for a quick bite to eat. But remember, you are not at the lab. You have not worked at the lab for nearly fifty years. You are at Belavista. Belavista is your last stop. The end of the line. What line? you may ask. The line that began, all those years ago, with the happy event of your birth. *It's a girl!* Do not, however, despair. Soon, Belavista will come to seem like your home and your Memory Team, like your "second family." Soon, in fact, you will forget your "first family" altogether and it will seem as if you have always been here (and perhaps, in some cosmic way, you *have*). Soon, in fact, you will be home.

AT UNEXPECTED MOMENTS the fear may suddenly hit you. You may find yourself lying wide awake late one night worrying that the kitchen will run out of crumb cake. Or that your husband has forgotten to defrost the meatloaf. *He'll starve!* Or that your last remaining sweater, the blue cable knit with the two leaping stags that you always loved to hate—"It's so *ugly*!"—will never come back from the laundry. You may worry that you forgot to keep a journal (you should have kept track of all those years). Or that your daughter needs new shoes. Or that your roommate, whom you have come to care for in ways you cannot explain—"She just lies there all day long doing *nothing*"—will suddenly be taken away in the middle of the night. You may worry that you are in the wrong room. The wrong bed. The wrong life. That life outside is rolling right along without you (it is). That you are not wanted (you are wanted). That you are not well (you are not well). That you are not missed (but you are, more than you will ever know).

AS THE DAYS slip by you will begin to forget more and more. Your terrible childhood during the war. All the beautiful gardens of Kyoto. The smell of rain in April. What you just ate for breakfast. *Cream of Wheat, with sausage links and toast.* The car accident, forty-three years ago, that killed your favorite cousin, Roy. You will forget the day you first met your husband. *I was sure he'd be gone in a week.* The perfect baby you wanted so badly. The damaged child that you got instead. All those laps you swam day after day, year after year, in the pool. You will forget the words for bicycle. Fish. Stone. The color of grass. *Sounds like stream.* And with each memory shed you will feel lighter and lighter. Soon you will be totally empty, a void, and, for the first time in your life, you will be free. You will have attained that state of being aspired to by mindful meditators across the planet—you will be existing utterly and completely "in the now."

EVERY ONCE IN a while, however, you may have a good day or even a good week. The fog will lift. The memories will return. Your jumbled thoughts will mysteriously, inexplicably reassemble themselves into coherent, syntactically correct sentences. *Whose room am I in, anyway?* And your family—*Hallelujah!*—will rejoice. *The medication is working!* In two or three weeks, they predict, you'll be back to your old self. Or maybe—it could happen—you are the one person in ten thousand who was misdiagnosed. *It was a vitamin D deficiency all along!* Do not be fooled. Your "improvement" is fleeting and temporary. Your decline has only momentarily stalled. You have reached what we here at Belavista like to call a "plateau." Tomorrow, or next week, or even a few minutes from now, you will resume your downward cognitive trajectory and the fog will once more descend.

WHAT ELSE CAN you expect? With time, your eyes will become dull, glazed, glassy, empty and then, eventually, blank. Your bones will grow thin, your hair, brittle. Your teeth, if you still have them, will turn yellow and then brown. They will be brushed only occasionally. No one will remember to floss under your bridges. *All that expensive dental work down the drain.* Your voice will grow hesitant. Your sentences will begin to flag. And then, one day, in an instant, which no one, not even the Memory Minder who knows you best, can predict, you will have spoken your last word. It might be "Yes," or "Juice!" Or you may simply smile, blink three times and then say, with a shrug, "Huh." And that's it, no one will ever hear from you again. *She's gone down the road,* we say. That day, however, is still a long ways off.

"WHY AM I here again?" you may find yourself asking us on occasion. And kindly, gently, we will remind you. Because your husband began noticing lately that you "just weren't yourself." *Then who could I be?* you asked him. Because when the doctor shot you up with radioactive dye, your PET scan lit up like a Christmas tree. Because your MRI came back riddled with lesions. Because you woke up one morning and your mind just felt "wrong." Because, after nine months, your family finally got the call. *There's a bed.* Because, like everyone else, you, too, got old. *Your turn*. Because, as we mentioned to you earlier, you failed the test. *Because*.

BY SIGNING BELOW you acknowledge that you have understood, to the best of your ability, everything we have just told you and agree to be bound by our terms and conditions. If you have any questions, please write them down on the blank page attached and a member of your Memory Team will get back to you as quickly as possible. Questions you may ask include What is today's date? (See Reality Orientation whiteboard.) What's the weather like outside? (See window.) And, What's for snack? (Melba toast with cottage cheese.) Questions you may not ask include Who took the children? (The children have not been taken.) Is this all there is? (Next question, please.) What happens when I leave here? (Your name will be deleted from our database.) And, What will they say about me when I'm gone? ("An avid swimmer," "A not-so-great driver," "A terrific mother," "The light of my life.")

WE HOPE THAT you enjoy your stay with us, and thank you again for choosing Belavista.

EURONEURO

What was it, you wonder, that first made her begin to forget? Was it the chemical in the hair dye that once turned her scalp bright red for two weeks? Was it something toxic in the hair spray (Aqua Net) that she used two and sometimes three times a day for more than thirty years? *Hold your breath!* she'd say as she pressed down on the nozzle and disappeared beneath a cloud of cold white mist. Was it the Raid that she sprayed all over the kitchen counter the minute she saw an ant? Was it sporadic? Genetic? A series of mini strokes? Something in the drinking water? The aluminum-laden antiperspirant? Too little sleep (she had been complaining about your father's snoring ever since the day they got married)? Too much TV? A dearth of hobbies? *Hobbies,* she once said to you, *who has time for hobbies?* Should she have eaten more blueberries? Less butter? Read more books? Read even one book (you don't remember ever seeing her read a single book, although there was always, piled high, on her nightstand, beside the mountain of stray socks, a stack of books she *meant* to read: *I'm OK, You're OK; How to Talk to Your Teenager; Teach Yourself French in One Week*)? Was it the hormone replacement after menopause? The estradiol? The Provera? The high blood pressure? The medication for the high blood pressure? Her undiagnosed thyroid condition? The deep and lingering depression she fell into the year after her mother died three days shy of one hundred and one? *Now what am I supposed to do?* she'd said. Was it *you?*

YOU RARELY CALLED. You never had children (and, except for a brief five-month period during your forty-fourth year—*too late!*—following the sudden and unexpected breakup with a man to whom you had been briefly engaged, you never wanted children). You left home early and moved to a faraway city from which you hardly ever returned, and when you did you went straight to your childhood bedroom (later hers) and quietly closed the door, which she opened five minutes later and at regular five-minute intervals throughout the rest of your brief but exhausting visit to tell you the latest news: whose husband had committed suicide by drinking a gallon of gin in a rented room at the Motel 6 in Ventura, who had just declared bankruptcy, who had become accidentally pregnant for the first time at the age of forty-nine (*So there's still hope!*), whose daughter had been rescued from a small rubber dinghy in Micronesia after being adrift on the Pacific for two and a half days (*She survived on nothing but cough drops and rainwater!*), who had fibroids, gout, twins, a tumor, a melanoma, an utter and complete breakdown that left her standing, naked, in the rain, in a parking lot at Carl's Jr., shaking her fist up at the sky at three in the morning and shouting, *Is there anybody there?* You found her overwhelming. Unnerving. Entrancing. Appalling. *Give that woman a tranquilizer!* your ex-husband said to you the first time he met her.

(AND ABOUT HIM, she later said, correctly, the day after he left you: *You were looking at him more than he was looking at you.*)

THE DAY AFTER he drives your mother to the home (her last ride), your father asks the housekeeper, Guadalupe, not to wash the sheets on her bed. "Please wait until next week," he says. Guadalupe, who was always very fond of your mother (your mother hired her eighteen years ago, before she began to forget) and whose own mother used to come with her every Monday morning to help clean the house until she was diagnosed with stage four metastatic breast cancer at the age of forty-six ("There *is* no stage five," your mother had reminded you), says, "Yes, Mr. Paul. I understand." The following week, he asks her again not to make up the bed. And the week after that. And so your mother's bed (once yours) remains unmade. A strand of her hair, still dark (Clairol Nice'n Easy, natural black), lies on the pillow. The pillow—unfluffed—still holds the shape of her head. At the foot of her bed, half hidden, are her ratty pink slippers (she took her good ones with her to the home).

HER FIRST FEW days there, the nurse tells you, your mother wandered up and down the halls, knocking on doors, peering into closets, looking under beds, calling out for your father. Her panic, at being left alone. After a while, though, she began to settle down.

Every day now she says the same thing: "My husband is coming to pick me up tomorrow."

OVER THE PHONE your father tells you that he, too, finds himself looking for her. Whenever he walks past her bedroom he pokes in his head to see if she's there. Sometimes he wakes up in the middle of the night and pats the bed beside him, "just to make sure," even though it has been more than six years since they shared the same bed, and even though he knows she's not there. Sometimes he hears her calling out to him from the other end of the house, or the quick patter of her slippers on the carpet outside his door. Last night he thought he saw her standing in the kitchen in her faded blue apron, washing a pile of dirty dishes at the sink. And for a moment everything was all right. (But, you want to say to him, she hated those dishes, that apron, that sink. And then you wonder: Without your mother in the kitchen, who is he? *An old man in an empty house.*)

YOU FIND HER sitting quietly in the Day Room by the window that looks out onto the street, watching the children walk home from school. Her hands are neatly folded, like two birds, in the shallow dip of her lap. Her nails are clean. Her hair is pressed flat to her head. She seems calm, possibly sedated. As soon as she sees you, however, she becomes so excited she almost begins to cry. "You came!" she says. And then she lowers her voice to a whisper. "I'm so embarrassed. I can hardly wait to get in the car and go home."

THERE HAD BEEN, of course, the usual early signs, which you had chosen to ignore. The jar of Pond's Cold Cream in the freezer. The repeatedly burnt rice. The pot of boiling water left unattended on top of the stove (and the accompanying bits of scorched and exploded egg your father had patiently scraped off the ceiling). The slightly unfocused smile. The extra fraction of a second—so brief as to be barely noticeable, but for that brief moment you knew you did not exist—it took her to recognize your voice whenever you called on the phone. The pile of half-written Christmas cards you found strewn across the card table on December 26—*Another year has passed!* they all began, but that was as far as she got—and the phone calls that started coming in that day and continued all throughout the next day and the next week and the entire month of January: "Alice, are you all right?" "Just wanted to make sure you're still alive." "Everything okay?" Yes, yes, your mother had said, she was fine, everything was fine, she was just feeling a bit . . . *tired.* Even though by then she had stopped cooking. She had stopped shopping. She had stopped swimming. She had stopped putting away her clothes and instead tossed them every night across the back of her faded pink wingback chair, which was soon no longer recognizable as a chair. And then, one day, you noticed, she had stopped cleaning her glasses. The lenses were smudged with greasy fingerprints. The frames were bent and uneven. How, you asked her, could she even *see* out of those things? Followed by—you couldn't help yourself—*You look like a crazy person!*

BUT YOU DIDN'T know. How could you have known? Because, for the longest time, she could still calculate the tip on the check at the Chinese restaurant—Fu Yuan Low—that she and your father went to in the mall every Sunday night at six (twenty percent rounded up to the nearest dollar and if it was Fay, their favorite waitress, twenty-five percent). She could still remember your birthday. She could still remember your brother's birthday. And the birthday of your other brother, the one who, after more than thirty-nine years (the *baby*), could still not remember anyone else's birthday but his own. She could remember the combination of her first bicycle lock. *Six, fifteen, thirty-nine.* And the license plate of the used '49 Ford she had bought in 1954 for five hundred dollars—*a fortune*—when she got her first paycheck from the hospital. She could remember the address of the new doctor she had visited earlier that morning with your father, she could remember the new doctor's suite number, the new doctor's telephone number, the name of the new doctor's receptionist, what the new doctor's receptionist had been wearing (*She looked just like a tramp!*). All these things she could still remember.

SO WHAT IF SHE watered your father's favorite orchid four and five times a day, causing its sudden and premature death and a small flood—a puddle, really—on the mahogany dining room table? *We'll just buy another one,* your father had said (Did he mean the orchid plant or the dining room table? You can't remember. Both, probably!). So what if she insisted upon making up her own rules while driving. *I turn on red no matter what!* So what if she asked you three times in fifteen minutes if you needed more underwear (always, she was thinking of you) or told the same story five times in a row (*The Kawahashis' daughter has married a Mormon!*) or occasionally misspelled your name? What was an extra vowel or two anyway? Or a consonant gone missing?

THE NEW DOCTOR had said it wasn't Alzheimer's. If it was Alzheimer's, he said, she wouldn't have remembered the trip to Costco the week before with your father, or her upcoming lunch date at the Olive Garden with her good friend Jane ("I can hardly wait!"). It was frontotemporal dementia. FTD. Some of the symptoms: gradual changes in personality, inappropriate behavior in public, apathy, weight gain, loss of inhibition, the desire to hoard. When your father asked for the prognosis, the new doctor—a soft-spoken former violin prodigy from Israel who was reputed to be "one of the best"—had clasped his hands on his desk and then sighed. It was terminal, he said. Atrophy of the frontal lobe. "Ravel had it."

~~~~~~
~~~~~~

FOR YEARS, SHE had lived in anticipation of The Big One. Every night, before she went to bed, she checked to make sure that the earthquake latches were fastened shut on all the kitchen cupboard doors. *My dishes!* She stockpiled food in the pantry: cans of minestrone soup, creamed spinach, tins of Spam, bags of *senbei* rice crackers, miniature jars of Mauna Loa macadamia nuts, her disaster food of choice. Because you never knew. You had to be prepared! Calamity could strike at any time of day or night (the car that swerves in front of you at the very last minute, the knock on the door in the early hours before dawn: *Open up!*). And now, finally, The Big One was here.

SHE BEGAN STUFFING Kleenex into her bra every morning so her nipples wouldn't show. She insisted upon drinking her coffee out of the same dirty Styrofoam cup day after day. She became fixated on trucks (they were terrible), the news on TV (there was *no good news* anymore), unruly children in restaurants (it was all the parents' fault), red lights (she hated them), police cars (they should be *banned*). When her cousin Harriet took her to Catalina Island for the weekend the painted buffalo statues on Avalon's main street drove her crazy. "These things are *awful!*" In the grocery store, whenever she saw someone who looked like herself—small, older, black-haired, slanted eyes—she made a beeline for them and asked, "Excuse me, but do I know you?" Usually, they would look at her and ask: "Do I know *you?*" But that was as far as the conversation went.

ALWAYS, THE DESIRE to be with "her own."

THE WOMAN ON the other side of the curtain is Vietnamese. Her face is beautiful, unlined. Her hair is jet black. She never leaves her bed. She never has any visitors. She never says a word. Mostly, she sleeps. "Ninety-three years old," the nurse tells you. "I don't think she's going to make it," your mother says. She takes two pills from a tiny paper cup and then swallows. "When I get better," she tells you, "we can go shopping at Nordstrom's. I'll buy you a new dress." Outside the window a young woman in the parking lot is pleading with her child to get out of the car. Your mother raps once on the glass pane and then turns to you. "Did you know you were fed by breast milk?" she asks.

FIVE DAYS A WEEK for four years she visited her own mother at the very same home. She flossed her teeth. She brushed her hair. She clipped her nails. She rubbed aloe vera lotion fortified with vitamin E onto her legs and feet and into the spaces between her toes. She read to her from the obituaries in the *Rafu Shimpo*. "Mrs. Matsue has died of complications of a stroke!" And every Friday, without fail, she brought her sweet bean *manju*—her favorite—from the Fugetsu-Do Bakery. "She took such good care of her," one of the aides tells you, "we didn't have to do a thing!"

YOU NEVER ONCE invited your mother to come visit you in all the years that you were away. You never wrote to her. You never called to wish her a happy birthday. You never took her to Paris or Venice or Rome, all places she had dreamed of one day seeing—*When your father retires*, she would say, but then, late last year, when he finally did retire, he was *too tired*—and all places you yourself have been to not once but several times, for a wedding, a honeymoon, a literary festival, an award ceremony, for the opening night of a theatrical production, in French, of your second novel, which you based on the most painful and difficult years of her life (she, on the other hand, took her then eighty-one-year-old mother on a ten-day "foliage tour" of New England the year you left for college: she bought the plane tickets, she rented the car, she booked the motels, she plotted out the long and winding route through three different states just as the leaves were beginning to peak and—even though she had never, except for once, for three years, during the war, been east of the San Joaquin River—she *drove*). When she asked you why you weren't closer you said you didn't know. You closed the door. You turned your back. You grew quiet and still, like an animal. You broke her heart. And you wrote.

AND NOW, NOW that you've finally come home, it's *too late* (your friend Carolyn just took her mother on a two-week cruise to Alaska and said it was *the best experience of her life*).

THROUGH THE DOORWAY you can see her hunched over a round Formica table in the Activities Room with some of the other residents, tracing the outline of a bunny onto a fluted paper plate. Above her, on the wall, the television is blaring. You tap her once on the shoulder from behind and she stops what she is doing and looks up at you. "A five-year-old could do this!" she says. And then she resumes tracing. A few seconds later she stops again. "Your hair's too dry," she says. And then: "Where's your father?"

WHENEVER THE PHONE rings and it's somebody asking for your mother or the lady of the house, your father says she can't come to the phone, which is true. And then he offers to take a message, which he writes down in his illegible scrawl in the red spiral notebook he keeps by the toaster on the kitchen counter. *Call dentist to schedule your next cleaning!* Or he'll tell the caller that your mother is out, which is also true, although not as true as she's out *forever*. Sometimes he answers on the very first ring, terrified that it's the home and something awful has happened—your mother has fallen in the shower and shattered her hip, she's choked on her lunch, she's hysterical and crying and wants to come home (*I promise I'll behave!*)—but more and more now he lets the phone ring until the answering machine picks up and her voice comes over the line. *We're sorry, we can't come to the phone right now . . .* Another reason he doesn't like to answer the phone is because of his accent (*Harro?*), which you never even realized he had (*Congraturation!*) until you invited a classmate home one day from school (why, she asked, did your father give you a name he can't even pronounce?). Half the time, the person on the other end of the line has no idea what your father is saying, and one time out of ten, that person hangs up. It was always your mother (no accent) who answered the phone.

WHEN HE WAS a young boy, your father once told you, he had a pair of songbirds (he couldn't remember their name in English), which he kept in a bamboo cage by the stove. This was many years ago, in the tiny mountain village in Japan. The birds sang from morning until night and every once in a while one of them laid a perfect speckled egg. One day, one of the birds—he didn't know which one, they looked exactly alike—died. The other bird stopped eating and became very thin. The house grew quiet. He put the bird near the window so it could hear the wild birds singing outside, but still it would not eat. Day after day it sat on its perch with its head down, growing thinner and thinner, until he was sure it was going to die. One morning he woke to the sound of the bird chirping again. His mother had hung a small round mirror inside the cage and now the bird was standing erect on its perch, singing to its reflection in the glass. It began to eat again and lived for another nine years.

WHAT DID THE bird see in the mirror? you now wonder. Its dead mate or its own reflection? Or were they one and the same? (When your father first told you this story, however, your response had been quite different. "Stupid bird!" you'd said. You were eight years old and had just completed the third grade.)

VALENTINE'S DAY. On the way to visit your mother, your father wants to stop off at Safeway to buy her a dozen red roses (something he never did "before"). When you walk into her room she looks at him and then she turns away. She doesn't look at you at all. "Do you know who this man is?" the nurse asks her. "Of course I do, he's my husband," your mother answers. "Don't let that smile fool you," she adds. When your father steps out of the room to go look for a vase, your mother leans toward you and whispers, "He's getting old."

SHE LOOKS DOWN at her hands quite often now, and at first you cannot figure out why. Then, one day: "Where's my wedding ring?" (Behind the tissue box in the top drawer of your father's nightstand.)

HER HOPES WERE once extravagant. She wanted perfect babies with straight black hair and a nice house with a fireplace and a big backyard where the children could run and play. After two tries, one disastrous (the arteries in the baby's heart were transposed), and the other not, she got the perfect baby (you), followed by two more ("the boys," each perfect in his own way), she got the nice house (albeit tract), she got the fireplace (with cozy gas flame) and the big-enough yard (swing set, cherry tree, brick pond filled with koi). Now all she wants is to be in the car with your father. "Wouldn't it be nice to go for a drive and I could navigate?" she asks him as he is getting up to leave. "You could let me be your guide."

THE NEXT DAY, she tells the nurse: "No more eggs, so sex is over."

A MEMORY FROM before. Spring cleaning. You are helping her go through her drawers and get rid of the things she no longer needs: an old corset, the metal stays bent and rusted, a filthy white "flair" hairbrush with half the bristles missing (you own an identical and equally filthy hairbrush in a similar state of disrepair, which you cannot, no matter how hard you try, make yourself get rid of—she bought it for you one afternoon, thirty-five years ago, from the Avon lady who came knocking at the door), a rubber girdle, a broken plastic Minnie Mouse watch, something—a hot-water bottle? an enema bag?—you cannot quite place ("It's a douche bag!" your father shouts out from the other side of the room), a round pink plastic case, inside of which you find a diaphragm. You hold it out to her. "Toss or keep?" *If I get pregnant again I'll scream!* she says. From the back of her closet you pull out an ancient white lab coat from Alta Bates Hospital. *Toss it!* A red Chinese silk jacket with blue and gold embroidered flowers given to her by her friend, Mrs. Fong, from the pool. *It's junk! Toss it!* A pair of Pappagallo pumps with peekaboo toes, the heels ground down to stumps. *Garbage!* The blue pin-striped blazer she bought at I. Magnin the week before your college graduation. *I'll never wear it again!* A cheap polyester blouse she bought on sale at Mervyn's ages ago, with the tags still attached (FINAL SALE, FIFTY PERCENT OFF). *Keep that,* she says, *I might need it one day for the assisted-living facility.* And then she begins to laugh. And so do you. Because it's a joke! She didn't really mean it! She was *just kidding.*

TODAY WHEN YOU visit her she is wearing the polyester blouse from Mervyn's and a pair of dark green stretch pants you do not recognize ("community property," you later learn). The nurses have brushed her hair and dabbed her cheeks with rouge. "I've been waiting for you," she says. Beside her, on the bed, is a pillowcase stuffed with her clothes. "They're sending me home today." On the other side of the half-drawn curtain the Vietnamese woman is snoring softly, her mouth wide open, one alarmingly thin arm flung carelessly across the top of the sheets at an odd angle, as though she had been dropped from the sky. "I wish she would wake up," your mother says. You begin taking her clothes out one by one from the pillowcase and putting them back in her drawers. "Here," she says, "let me help you." And she shows you how to properly fold a blouse.

YOUR FATHER HANGS on to little things. When she writes down her own name (for the last time, it turns out), this is cause for celebration. At least, he says, she can still write. At least she can still read. At least she can still tell the time. At least she can still feed herself. At least she still knows who he is. At least she still knows who *she* is when she sees her own face in the bathroom mirror (smart bird!). When he reads an article in *Scientific American* about a drug that stops the buildup of abnormal protein deposits in the brain cells of old mice, he can hardly wait to tell you. "They're going to find a cure!"

YOU ALWAYS THOUGHT she would live forever. She never got sick. She never complained. She never broke a single bone. She was, for as long as you can remember, as "strong as an ox." She could open any jar, twist off any cap, close any suitcase (*Here, let me do it!*). Her arches were high. Her legs were fabulous (at the dance hall, her cousin once told you, she could always find your mother by her legs). Her face was smooth and unblemished. For years, not a single wrinkle. Whenever you went out to a restaurant, people would compliment your father on his four beautiful children. They thought your mother was your older sister (the one you should have had).

EVERY HALLOWEEN YOUR brother used to dress up as her. The flouncy crinoline poodle skirt. The beaded cashmere sweater with the fake pearl buttons. The flamingo pink lipstick. The nylon stockings (Lively Lady, all nude). The navy blue pumps stuffed with newspapers, to accommodate his tiny feet. He was an exceptionally beautiful child. More beautiful than your mother, even. More beautiful than you! He had enormous black eyes and a full head of dark curly hair—*You must have run off with the milkman!* people said to your mother—that he liked to wear long. Everyone thought he was a girl. But then, out came the little boy voice: "*Boo!*" You, on the other hand, looked more like your father. The thin, narrow lips. The high forehead. The square, workmanlike hands. Every Halloween, you dressed up as a turtle.

~~~~~~~
~~~~~~~

YOUR FATHER DRIVES alone around town now in his old brown Buick. To the gas station, to the barbershop, to the supermarket, down the hill to the home, to visit your mother, wearing his Members Only jacket. "Her" car, the blue one, he takes out for a drive once a week to keep the engine running. Sometimes the neighbors are surprised to see him behind the wheel. *Where's Alice?*

LITTLE BY LITTLE, she is beginning to disappear. Her hair is thinning on top and her mouth now hangs slightly askew. But the minute you walk into the lunchroom—a sea of elderly women and the occasional stray old man, looking bewildered and alone (*Just ten minutes ago I was running through the grass!*)—her eyes light up and you break out into a big smile. When you get to her table, however, you realize you've been smiling at a stranger. It's the wrong mother. *Not yours!* Your mother is seated at the next table over, quietly eating her lunch off a faded yellow fiberglass tray. She still eats like a lady, slowly raising and lowering her fork to her lips, taking her time between bites, chewing thoroughly, thoughtfully, now and then dabbing at the corners of her mouth with a white paper napkin, wiping away an errant crumb. No rush. She takes a sip of milk through a striped plastic straw (you don't remember ever seeing her drink milk before) and then she looks at you. "Are you still a virgin?" she asks.

AT NIGHT, YOUR father still sleeps on "his" side of the bed. The sheets on "her" side remain smooth and unruffled, the bedspread pulled taut. Magazines begin to pile up on his dresser. *Reader's Digest, Oprah, Better Homes & Gardens, Family Circle.* Unopened envelopes from the *Harvard Women's Health Watch* newsletter litter his desk. He decides to send away for the special *Harvard Women's Health Watch* newsletter binder. Nine ninety-five for a piece of plastic. He orders six of them and fills them with back issues of the newsletter (your mother has saved them all), which no one will ever read.

THE YELLOW POST-IT NOTES are still scattered all throughout the house. On the refrigerator in the kitchen: *Don't forget to take your pills.* Above the telephone: *Never give out credit card info.* On the bathroom mirror: *Did you turn off the faucet?* On your mother's bedroom mirror: *Chin up!* Lying facedown on the nightstand beside her bed is her old week At-a-Glance planner, in which she has written the same entry day after day, week after week, in her tiny, ladylike handwriting: *Do not cross out tomorrow!* (She never did.) Your father puts away the week At-a-Glance in his desk drawer. He tosses—finally, after months—her dirty nightgown into the hamper. But he leaves up the Post-it notes. Just in case she gets better and they decide to send her home. "I wouldn't want her to get confused."

THE DAY AFTER her mother died, your mother took to her reclining chair in the "family room" and refused to get up. She was despondent. Dispirited. Enraged. She'd let her mother down. It was somehow *all her fault*. But, your father reminded her, her mother was *one hundred one years old*. "One hundred," your mother corrected him. She should have used her walker more. Taken that Memory Works class. Gone to balloon badminton. Signed up for chair yoga. And then, over and over again, *How could this have happened?*

THREE WEEKS LATER your father called to tell you he was worried. "Your mother just sits in that chair eating cookies and watching TV all day long," he said. But, he had to admit, she'd had a difficult few years, driving down to the home to see her mother five days a week. Who could blame her for needing a rest? He would give her until the one-year anniversary of her mother's death to "get her bearings" and then he would "give her a nudge," but the one-year anniversary came and went and your mother stayed put in her chair.

ANOTHER MEMORY FROM before: your mother, sitting on the edge of her bed, head down, hands dangling between her legs, shoulders slumped. Utter defeat. "What's wrong?" you asked her. Your mother, who had always been a stylish dresser, eyebrows plucked, makeup perfectly applied, "never a hair out of place." Your mother, who had groomed you (every morning, before you went to school, she fixed the barrette in your hair "just so"), shopped for you (*Here, try this!*), threaded the bobbin on her old black Singer sewing machine and stayed up until late in the night sewing for you (gingham blouses, Western-style shirts with snap pockets and classic double yokes, your first wraparound skirt, a midi dress with V-neck—low but not *too* low!—and drawstring puff sleeves, a halter top with custom-fitted "darts"), could no longer put on her pants. *What do I do with the zipper?* she asked you.

MAYBE THIS IS where it all began.

HER FIRST CHRISTMAS at the home. You bring her the gifts you and your father spent the evening before wrapping at the kitchen table while listening to Mahalia Jackson (her favorite) on the radio. When you ask her if she'd like to open the present from your father first, she says, "No." You give her one of your presents instead, a small box containing a dragonfly good luck charm. She holds the box up to the nurse. "See?" she says. "This is how much she loves me. She gives me tiny presents." When she opens your father's gifts—five pairs of socks, an argyle sweater, a plush terry-cloth bathrobe, a jar of mixed nuts, a pair of lamb's wool slippers with soft leather soles—she says, "He's giving me so many presents, trying to get on my good side." The following Saturday, when you call, you remind her that your father will be stopping by later that afternoon to see her. "I don't think he misses me," she says.

ONE NIGHT, SEVERAL years ago, when they still shared the same bed, your father's snoring was so loud—"He sounded just like a lion!"—that your mother got up and went to go sleep in your room. After a while, though, she came back. "I got lonely." The next night she went again to your room, only this time she slept straight through until morning. After that, there was no going back. *You can get used to anything.*

YOU NEVER ONCE remember seeing your parents touch. You never saw them kiss. You never saw them hold hands. You never observed a single gesture of tenderness between them. And yet, when your father began getting urinary tract infections and he and your mother went to the urologist to find out why, the doctor quickly stepped out of the exam room, quietly closed the door behind him, then burst back into the room a moment later with an enormous grin on his face and said, "Sex!" (*Boo!*) Every time your mother told you this story, and she told it often, she would burst out laughing.

THIS WAS THE first of the stories she began to repeat.

- - - - - - - -

THERE WAS ALSO the story about the carpool driver, Mrs. Mrozek, who forgot to pick up your three-year-old brother from the Little Red Nursery School at the bottom of the hill (a police officer found him a mile away, walking along a busy thoroughfare, calmly headed in the direction of home). And the time that your other brother, the lawyer, went after her boss, Dr. Nomura, when he tried to cheat her out of her 401(k) ("I told him, 'My son will see you in court!'"). And then, of course, there were the stories about "camp." The guard towers. The rattlesnakes. The barbed-wire fence. How her mother had killed all the chickens in the yard the day before they packed up the house and they left. "She snapped their necks one by one beneath the handle of a broomstick," your mother would say. And then she would end the story the way she always did, for the tenth time, for the fiftieth time, for the hundredth time: "It was a mess!"

HER MOTHER'S PHOTOGRAPH still stands atop the "dining hutch" in the dining room. Your father used to look at it and say, *Why didn't you teach your daughter how to cook?* (With the exception of rice, your mother only cooked "American": meatloaf, tuna casserole, macaroni and cheese, beef stroganoff made with sour cream and Campbell's cream of mushroom soup.) And whenever she yelled at him, your mother once told you, laughing, he would point to the photograph and say, *She's watching!*

ONE AFTERNOON, NOT long before she retired to her chair, your father woke up from a nap to find your mother had disappeared. He checked the backyard, the front yard, even the little garden shed where he kept all of his tools, but she was nowhere to be found. Finally he ran out into the street, calling her name, but there was no answer. When he returned to the house he opened the garage door and found her sitting in the passenger seat of the brown Buick, waiting to go for her ride. She had on her lipstick and her "outdoor" shoes and her purse was neatly placed on her lap. "Where were you?" she asked him.

TODAY, FOR THE first time, the Vietnamese woman is wide awake. She follows you with her eyes as you walk across the room and then she taps herself on the chest. "No English," she says. And then she smiles—her teeth are bright white, perfect, her eyes are dancing black orbs. "You, daughter?" she asks.

LATER, YOUR MOTHER says, "Didn't everything used to have a name?"

YOUR FATHER DOES things to pass the time. He reads the newspaper from cover to cover. He learns, and quickly masters, sudoku. He watches the solar eclipse through a tiny pinhole in a cardboard box. In April, he does his taxes. He plants new trees alongside the fence that borders the neighbor's backyard (always, his obsession with privacy). He apologizes to the dying rhododendron in the garden ("Even a worm an inch long," he once told you, "has a half-inch-long soul") and then swiftly cuts it down. He makes a halfhearted attempt to clean out—finally, after more than thirty years—*the garage*. He buys a pedometer and begins to walk. A half mile, a mile, a mile and a half. And then, one day, he decides to make a rock garden outside your mother's bedroom window. He orders three bags of white gravel from the Overlook Nursery and uses a system of levers, pulleys and ropes attached to the fence at its strongest and most stable point (before he taught math at the college, he was an engineer by training) to haul up seven large white rocks from the ravine behind the house. He takes his time—two or three days—arranging and re-arranging the rocks until they look "just right." What logic he uses, how he determines the spaces between them and their ideal configuration, you do not know ("Compared to the mother," your friend Anne's eight-year-old daughter once said to her, "the father is like a stranger"). He takes a Polaroid of the rock garden and brings it to the home to show your mother. "You killed the plants?" she asks him.

WHEN YOU COME back after a short trip abroad—a ten-day writers' conference in the south of Umbria—your father tells you that her left foot has begun to drag. They've put her in a wheelchair, he says, so as not to risk a fall. Already, after one week, her legs look thin as twigs. Also, she's much quieter. And she no longer smiles. This is the thing that bothers him most.

WHEN YOU WALK into her room she is sitting in her wheelchair by the window, holding up a small round mirror, staring intently, but with suspicion, at half of her face (every morning, when you were a child, you used to watch her "do her face" in front of the bathroom mirror). "I could never please my mother," she says. You take the mirror from her and place it facedown on the bed. Her chin is trembling and her hands feel cold as ice. You take them between yours to warm them up and she leans back in her wheelchair and closes her eyes. "Thank you," she says. Then she sits up and opens her eyes wide. "When you leave," she asks, "who will turn off the light?"

WHEN YOU WERE a child, whenever you felt sad she would tell you to "look in the mirror and smile." Other things she used to say: "If someone asks you, always let them play" (mostly, you did), "Never visit anyone without bringing a gift" (sometimes you forgot), "Always cut your carrots on the diagonal" (you still do) and "If you get married again without letting me know, boy are you in hot water!" (You eloped with your first husband, the ex–Zen monk, two weeks after meeting him at a six-day silent retreat up in the Catskills.) And about men in general: "You must pretend to take them seriously" and "It's not always about you!"

LITTLE GESTURES. Still, the impulse to be kind. At lunch, when the woman in the wheelchair beside her begins to weep, your mother reaches over and pats her hand. "Don't cry," she says.

THE NEXT TIME you visit her, the Vietnamese woman is gone. Her bed has been stripped and disinfected. Her belongings—what few she had—neatly disposed of into a large black plastic garbage bag. She died during her sleep, the aide tells you. By the end of the day a younger *hakujin* woman named Sarah has already taken her place. Sarah is in her late fifties, elegantly dressed, with neatly manicured nails and a wide, friendly smile. If you saw her pushing a cart through the grocery store, you think, you wouldn't look twice. Her vocabulary, however, consists of a single, tragic word: "tan." "Where's my friend?" your mother says. And then, for the rest of the visit, she is silent.

SHE ASKS FOR so little now. And whatever you do for her—straighten her glasses, open the juice carton, wipe away a crumb from her face with a napkin, smooth down her hair—she says, softly but clearly, "Thank you."

ENJOY YOURSELF WHILE YOU CAN, she used to say to you, *because once you hit fifty it's one repair job after another!* You are about to "hit" fifty, and already the repair jobs have begun: the physical therapy for your frozen shoulder, the elimination of a trio of suspicious moles, the orthotics for your plantar fasciitis, the acupuncture—*useless!*—for your aching, arthritic knee. After your latest doctor's appointment—the GI, for the pain you get in your stomach every time you begin to eat—you resolve to take better care of yourself. From now on, you will take the stairs up and not just down. You will renew your membership at the gym. You will dust off your mantra and take up meditation again. You will stop smoking. Lose weight. Improve your diet. Give up meat. Dairy. Coffee. Lay off the salted pretzels. You will become a vegan. A virgin! A yoga person. An outdoor person (*You can't stay in your room forever!* your mother used to say to you, even though, with the exception of your brief foray into married life, you basically *have*—you are, after all, a writer). You will walk down to the ocean every morning at dawn and lift your arms to the sky and then, slowly, reverently, with gratitude and awe, you will bow down to the ground and salute the rising sun. *One more day.*

SHE NO LONGER looks out the window. She no longer asks for your father. She no longer asks when she is going home. Sometimes, days go by and she doesn't say a thing. Other days all she can say now is "yes."

"Are you feeling all right?"

"Yes."

"Is the new medicine helping?"

"Yes."

"Does anything hurt?"

"Yes."

"Do you like it here?"

"Yes."

"Are you lonely?"

"Yes."

"Do you still dream of your mother?"

"Yes."

"Is my blouse too tight?"

"Yes."

"If there is one thing you could tell me what would it be?"

Silence.

FROM TIME TO TIME, flashes of her old self reemerge. "Did you like having brothers?" she asks you one day (you tell her that you loved it). And then, for the next five months, not a word.

THE LAST COMPLETE sentence she ever utters is "It's a good thing there's birds."

DAY BY DAY your father is slowly losing his hearing. "No one to talk to," he says. Sometimes he imagines your mother is outside in the garden, watering the roses to death. Or maybe she's fallen asleep in front of the television with her mouth wide open, one half-slippered foot dangling precariously over the edge of the padded footrest. Or maybe she has wandered next door to invite over the new neighbors—again!—to come see the view, even though they have the same view from their backyard as your parents do from theirs, only transposed by seventy-five feet. Or maybe she is her old self again and has gone out to buy groceries—*There's a sale on rib roast at Vons!*—and any minute now he'll hear the familiar sound of her car in the driveway. *Honk, honk!*

YOU ARE SITTING with her in the Quiet Room, she in her wheelchair, you on the sofa beside her, listening to the steady patter of rain on the white noise machine. You have not heard the sound of her voice, now, in almost two years. Suddenly, she reaches out and grasps your arm. Her grip is strong but gentle. Her hand is unexpectedly warm. Your mother, you realize, is *holding* you. And for the first time in weeks you feel calm. *Don't stop.* You stay like that, she with her hand on your arm, you on the sofa beside her, not moving, barely breathing, for several minutes, until it is time to wheel her into the Dining Room for lunch. The best five minutes of your life.

EVERY TIME YOU leave you bend over and give her a kiss. Sometimes she pulls away. Other times she looks at you and offers up an indifferent cheek. Always, as you are walking away—you can't help yourself—you turn around and look back. Sometimes she is watching you, but she doesn't seem to recognize your face. Sometimes she is gazing off into space. Sometimes she is leaning over in her wheelchair and staring down, intently, with fierce concentration, at the top of her feet. She has already forgotten you. Today, however, when you turn around and look back, her hand is half raised in midair and slowly waving goodbye.

THE FIRST THING you realize, the moment after she dies, is: you forgot to arrange for the brain autopsy. So you call the woman at Fukui Mortuary, who gives you the name of the pathologist, Wayne Kato, who, for a fee of fifteen hundred dollars, cuts open your mother's skull with an oscillating saw and carefully harvests her brain before hand-delivering it in a Styrofoam cooler packed with ice to the lab of the renowned neurologist Professor Muller, who, for a fee of thirteen hundred dollars, soaks it in formaldehyde for two weeks and then slices the tissue and stains it on slides. Her findings, you learn, when you call her to discuss the report, concur with the new doctor's: it wasn't Alzheimer's, it was frontotemporal dementia. Subtype Pick's disease. Pick's brains, the professor tells you, are quite rare. "We don't see too many of them." Your mother's brain, she adds, was "quite atrophic." In August the professor will present your mother's slides at an international neurology-neuropathology conference in Paris. "The EuroNeuro." When you ask her if she can send you a photograph of your mother's brain, she pauses. "No one's ever asked me that before," she says.

FOR THE FIRST time in your life, you cannot sleep. You try melatonin. You try Lunesta. Sonata. Intermezzo. You try Ativan. You try deep breathing. You try alternate nostril breathing. You try progressive muscle relaxation. You try repeating the word "peace" over and over again until it no longer sounds like a word. You try lettuce tea right before bedtime. You try a banana one hour before bedtime. You try no liquids after six. You try lavender oil. Aromatherapy. Heated blankets. Turning the thermostat down to sixty-three. You try Sleep Shepherd. Dream Team. Eye Slack. NightWave. Hushhhhh. But still, you cannot sleep.

YOUR FATHER ORDERS a CPAP machine and gets his first good night of sleep in years. No more waking up every five minutes and gasping for breath. No more snoring. No more dozing off during the eight-o'clock news ("Hey, sleepyhead!" your mother would say). Every morning now he wakes up feeling clear-headed and refreshed. "I should have done this ages ago," he tells you. A week later, he replaces the big bed in the "master bedroom" with a smaller adjustable bed that allows him to elevate his head to minimize the nightly upswell of acid reflux. He takes down the Post-it notes. *Don't forget to turn off the light!* She is not coming home.

TOGETHER YOU BEGIN sorting through her things. In her bathroom, you find: nine empty bottles of Shiseido foundation (natural light ivory), thirty-two tubes of lipstick, one electric toothbrush (every evening she would brush her teeth, put on her face cream and her Oil of Olay—"Maybe Dad will hold my hand!"—and *dive* into bed), a set of bleaching trays for whitening her teeth, two packages of adult diapers, three unopened bags of sanitary napkins she had been saving "just in case" ("I might use them someday"). All of this, of course, is *garbage*.

IN YOUR FATHER'S *den*, which at some point became your mother's *nest*, there are boxes and boxes of expired coupons, some more than fifteen years old (she prided herself on being a good shopper and would drive from one supermarket to the next—Safeway, Market Basket, Ralphs—to save fifty cents), hundreds of Ask Marilyn columns she had spent hours carefully cutting out of *Parade* magazine, old Martha Stewart columns ("Hot tips on the best way to store and display photos"), recipes from the newspaper that she never made, ancient sewing patterns from Simplicity and McCall's, faded scraps of fabric and "rickrack," assorted lengths of string, empty Cool Whip containers for storing the leftover rice, multiple Xerox copies of your first published short story, one of which she had slipped into a plastic Ziploc bag and brought with her to show the ladies in the locker room at the pool. *My daughter's a writer!* All of these things, too—*garbage.*

IN THE "GOOD SWEATER DRAWER" in her bedroom, you find: an old notepad containing the phone numbers and addresses of her three children (*They scattered to the wind*), a list of her children's favorite foods (one of your brothers liked Chinese paper-wrapped chicken, the other, shrimp scampi and you, you loved eel), a vegetarian cookbook (*The Vegetarian Epicure*) that she bought after you became a vegetarian during your freshman year of college (by your sophomore year, however, you had reverted to your natural carnivorous ways), an old rubber swim cap (with bright yellow daisy still intact), two well-worn packs of Bicycle playing cards (she always won at hearts), a red patent leather lipstick case (Coach) with inside mirror that you gave to her one Christmas, which she never appears to have used. You slip the list of favorite foods into your pocket. Everything else—*garbage*—you toss.

ON THE FLOOR of her closet are nineteen purses, all cheap, all brand-new. Your father points to one. "Save that," he says. It looks no different from any of the others. He'd like to keep it, he says, as a *souvenir*. You set it aside.

THE DAY BEFORE she flew out East to attend your college graduation, your mother packed her best jewelry—three black water pearl necklaces of differing lengths that her father had brought over with him on the boat from Japan—into a small brown suitcase. At the airport, while she was waiting for your father to park the car, two young men approached her and politely asked for directions. Your mother, always friendly, always eager to help, pointed them toward the ticket counter on the other side of the revolving glass doors. Five minutes later, when she reached down for her suitcase, it was gone. Your father was still circling around and around the terminal, looking for a place to park. "I wanted to give those pearls to you," your mother told you after the graduation ceremony. "They were your inheritance." (All the other things you should have inherited—your grandmother's Imari dishes, the ivory chopsticks, the antique wooden *tansu*, the set of Emperor and Empress dolls, the black-and-white photographs of your strange, kimono-wearing relatives in Japan—were destroyed in the first frenzy of forgetting, right after the start of the war.)

WHEN THEY RETURNED home your father drove her downtown to the jewelry district and let her pick out a few new pieces: a floral pearl brooch, a pair of clip-on ruby earrings, a sterling silver bracelet with her initials engraved, none of which she ever wore ("It's not the same"), and none of which you can find anywhere in the house. You've looked everywhere. And they're not there.

ONE LAST MEMORY. By the time you finish your third novel she has not spoken in more than one year. Now, your father says, he just wishes he could hear her say something, anything. But to whatever you ask, she just looks at you—her eyes calm, all-seeing, forsaken—and nods. You are not sure if she still knows who you are, so you write down your name on a name tag and pin it onto your shirt. You give her a copy of your book and watch her slowly leaf through the pages—her hands, though spotted, are still elegant, with long slender fingers that taper into perfect oval nails—and when she gets to your photograph on the back flap she stares intently at the picture of your face, then at your name printed beneath it, then at your name on the name tag pinned to your shirt, and then up at your face. And when she gets to your face, she stares into your eyes with wonder. She does this loop again and again. Photograph, your name beneath it, your name on your name tag, your face above it. And every time, when she gets to your face, she looks as if she is about to speak.

ACKNOWLEDGMENTS

Thank you to Nicole Aragi, for her tireless generosity and steering me right at every step of the way, and Jordan Pavlin, for believing in my work from the very beginning. Thank you, also, to Duvall Osteen, Maya Solovej, Isabel Yao Meyers, John Freeman, Max McDowell, Mark Horn, Dylan Leiner, Paul Wakenight, Mitchell Cohen and Lori Monson. Special thanks to David Otsuka, Michael Otsuka, Daryl Long and to my best friend, Kabi Hartman. The following works were also helpful to my research in the writing of this book: *Haunts of the Black Masseur* by Charles Sprawson; *Swim: Why We Love the Water* by Lynn Sherr; "A Feel for the Water" by Cynthia Gorney, *The New Yorker*; *Nobody's Home* by Thomas Edward Gass; *Old Friends* by Tracy Kidder; *Making Gray Gold* by Timothy Diamond; *Can't Remember What I Forgot* by Sue Halpern; *The Forgetting* by David Shenk. Finally, thank you, always, to Andy Bienen.

ALSO BY

JULIE OTSUKA

THE BUDDHA IN THE ATTIC

A gorgeous novel by the celebrated author of *When the Emperor Was Divine* that tells the story of a group of young women brought from Japan to San Francisco as "picture brides" nearly a century ago. In eight unforgettable sections, *The Buddha in the Attic* traces the extraordinary lives of these women, from their arduous journey by boat to their arrival in San Francisco and their tremulous first nights as new wives, from their experience raising children who would later reject their culture and language to the deracinating arrival of war. Once again, Julie Otsuka has written a spellbinding novel about identity and loyalty, and what it means to be an American in uncertain times.

Fiction

ALSO AVAILABLE
When the Emperor Was Divine